PRAISE FO

Amina: The Silent One

"Author Fiza Pathan prods our social conscience as she gives us an electric shock of delectable fiction."—Margaret Virany, author of *The Book of Kells: Growing Up in an Ego Void*

"Fast-paced and intense, this book is well plotted and will keep readers turning pages."—*The Booklife Prize*

"A powerfully gripping tale told by Fiza Pathan, *Amina: The Silent One* will fire up reader's emotions while bringing them to tears."—*Authors Talk About It*

"A truly remarkable work of fiction that touches heart and mind, *Amina: The Silent One* is sure to engender much thought and discussion."—*Book Viral*

"*Amina: The Silent One* by Fiza Pathan is one of the most socially relevant books on the market today in my opinion, and I highly recommend it. I could not put this book down. I was totally captivated throughout the entire story, and Amina and her family will be in my head, and on my heart for some time to come."—*Reader Views*

"Pathan paints a visceral image of slum life, and her likeable protagonist Amina helps to draw a reader in who might otherwise be ignorant to such an experience. The beautiful novel is an important read thanks to the issues it illustrates that so many women face not just in India, but in other parts of the world as well."—Extract from "6 Titles to Help Diversify Your Reads" by Joe Sutton for *IndieReader*

"Pathan has a captivating writing style. The characters she creates are totally real to the reader, and the world in which they live becomes very vivid too."—*Readers' Favorite*

"It feels as though she hasn't written a fictional story, but rather has pulled back the curtains on a grim reality to let the reader experience what it is like to have hope in a land in which despondency reigns."—*The US Review of Books*

"AMINA: THE SILENT ONE is a beautiful and thought-provoking novel that shines light on important issues facing women in India today."—*IndieReader*

Awards:

2015–2016 Reader Views Literary Awards — Global Award for Asia

2015–2016 Reader Views Literary Awards — Winner 1ˢᵗ Place General Fiction/Novel

2016 Readers' Favorite International Book Award — Bronze Medal

Foreword Reviews' 2015 INDIEFAB Book of the Year Award — Finalist Multicultural (Adult Fiction)

2015 New Apple Book Awards — Medalist Winner in E-book General Fiction

2016 Next Generation Indie Book Awards — Finalist Novella Category

Short-listed in the 2016 Book Viral Book Awards

55 Best Self-Published Books of 2015 — IndieReader

4th Annual Beverly Hills International Book Awards — Winner in Regional Fiction

2016 IAN Book of the Year Awards — Finalist General Fiction

2016 IAN Book of the Year Awards — Finalist Novella

2015 Pinnacle Book Achievement Award — Category Fiction

2015 New England Book Festival — Honorable Mention in Regional Literature

2016 Pacific Rim Book Festival — Runner-Up Regional Literature

2016 Hollywood Book Festival — Honorable Mention (Wild Card Entry)

2016 Great Midwest Book Festival — Runner-Up Regional Literature

Amina

The Silent One

Amina

The Silent One

Fiza Pathan

Fiza Pathan Publishing OPC Private Limited
Mumbai, India

Imprint: Freedom With Pluralism®
Fiza Pathan Publishing OPC Private Limited
Symbol Apartments, Flat No 2, Tertullian Road,
Off Dr. Peter Dias Road, Bandra West, Mumbai 400 050, India
E-mail: fizapathan@fizapathanpublishing.com
Website: www.fizapathanpublishing.ink

Publisher's Note: This is a work of fiction. Names, characters, places, and incidents are a product of the author's imagination. Locales and public names are sometimes used for atmospheric purposes. Any resemblance to actual people, living or dead, or to businesses, companies, events, institutions, or locales is completely coincidental.
Book Layout ©2017 BookDesignTemplates.com
Manuscript edited by Margaret Langstaff of Margaret Langstaff Editorial and Kimberly Catanzarite, www.editandproof.com
Cover Art.LLPix Photography & Design
Image: Sharvari Rane, licensed usage.
Lyrics of the song "At the Beginning with You" on Pg.124 are by Richard Marx from the movie *Anastasia* (Anastasia soundtrack/Atlantic Records). Lyrics of the song "Jai Maa Kali" on Pg. 138 are by Indeevar from the movie *Karan and Arjun.*

Book Title/ Author Name. Amina: The Silent One by Pathan, Fiza
ISBN 978-8-1936044-6-5 Hardback
ISBN 978-8-1936044-7-2 Paperback
ISBN 978-8-1936044-8-9 E-book

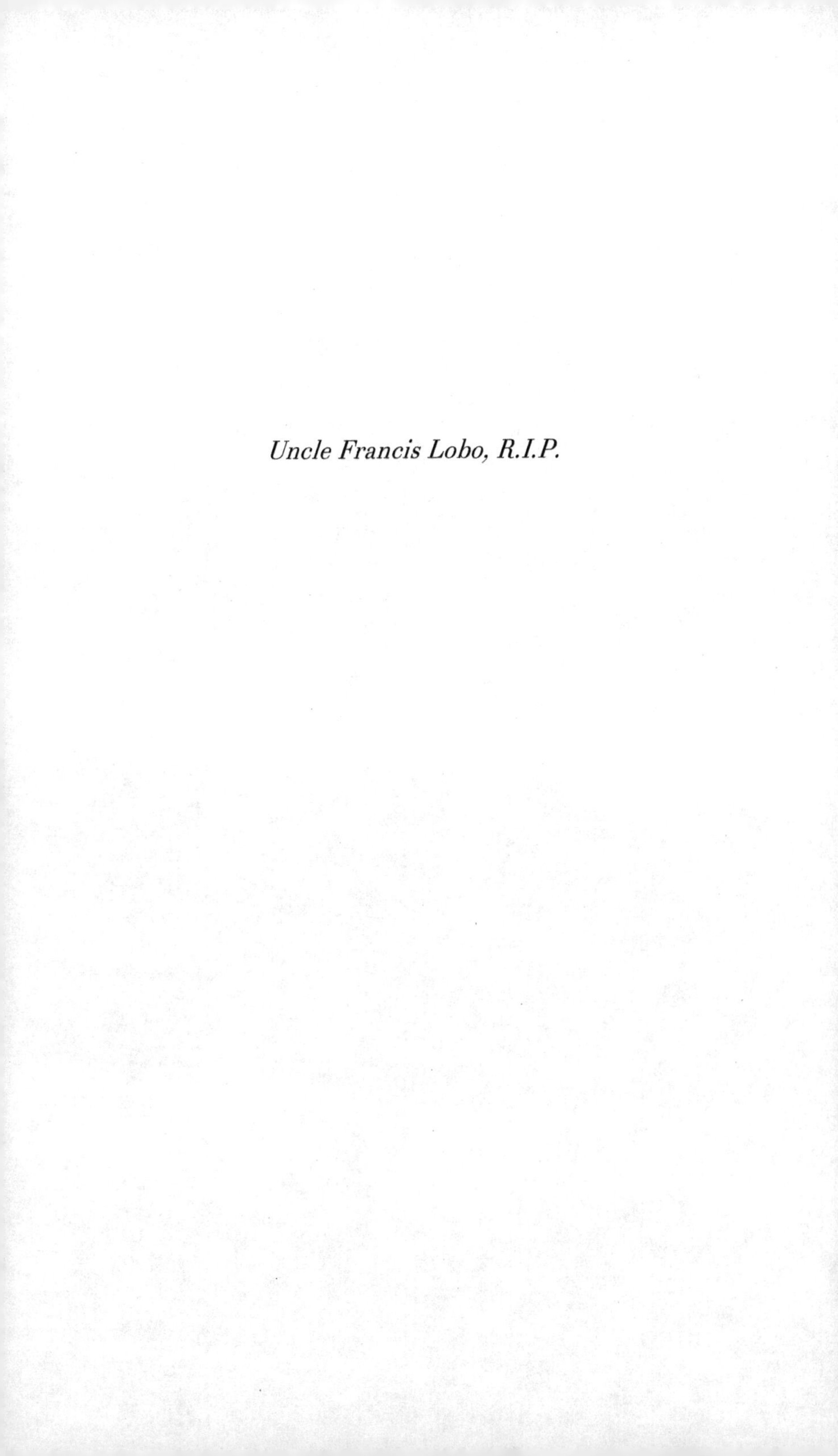

Uncle Francis Lobo, R.I.P.

Music acts like a magic key, to which the most tightly closed heart opens.

—Maria Augusta von Trapp

Khadijah was squatting on the floor as she chewed her betel leaves. The red juice filled up her cheeks and gave a nasty look to her already unbecoming face.

Her hand was placed upon her head as she watched her granddaughter Selma, aged six and a half, kneading the dough with her little fingers to make the chapattis for the whole family.

The old matron was about to spit her red betel juice out of the shanty, where her family stayed on the road, when she saw her son, the father of Selma, dragging his feet home. Khadijah rose to her feet clumsily before she spoke.

"Well, is it a boy?"

Her son, aged thirty, shook his head mournfully as he entered the two-room shanty made of steel plates and mud. He saw Selma struggling with the dough and becoming frustrated.

"No, ammijaan," he said.

"Oh no, Allah!" exclaimed the elderly woman, hitting her forehead with her left hand while the right one busily scratched her waist. "Not another girl. We already have two to feed and clothe!"

Selma looked up from her work. She was smiling a dimpled smile as she looked at her father, who sat down on the muddy earth near her.

"Abbujaan, mother has given birth to a girl ... wah, now I will have another sister to play with."

Khadijah hit the girl roughly on the head.

"Shut up, Selma, or I'll make you sweep the room again ... ya Allah," she bemoaned as she paced about the small shanty. "Ya Allah, why have you forsaken this family? We need a son, and you curse us with daughters, each one dumber than the next."

"I'm not dumb," whispered Selma, for which she got a kick in her belly from her grandmother. Jaffar, Khadijah's son, sat quietly looking at the image of the holy Kaaba nailed on the steel wall of the filthy shanty. Another girl ... another girl meant another ungainful mouth to feed ... another girl to get married ... another girl to get a dowry fixed for ... another girl.

Selma whimpered from her grandmother's blow. It was not the first she'd received, and it certainly wouldn't be the last. She, therefore, continued to knead the dough, mixing it with the tears that fell from her eyes.

*

Dr. Rahim Muhammad Sheikh, doctor in history, sat at his ancient desk correcting a Ph.D. student's thesis on the legend of the incarnation of Lord Krishna when he heard a knock on his wooden door.

"Jumman!" called the doctor. "Jumman, my lad, please open the door."

A little boy dressed in a sparkling white kurta, white pants, and a skullcap hastily entered the room. He was the adopted son of the doctor. The doctor was unmarried and alone in this world. More than anything else, he was married to his studies and work.

He continued to correct the thesis as he heard his adopted son carefully open the door.

The boy cried, "Abbu, there is a man called Jaffar at the door with his wife and a baby who is very tiny. Do I let them in?"

Dr. Rahim Muhammad Sheikh lived on Mohammad Ali Road in the bustling city of Mumbai. He lived in a two-storey stone building, built by the early British colonists in 1914. The house was neat, filled to capacity with books, paintings, and antiques from Egypt and Greece, and Chinaware and old photographs of the doctor's family, all arranged tidily. Jumman, the little-adopted boy, enjoyed living in that old worn-out home.

The doctor's home was old, but he was rich—his home so unlike the shanty made of cow dung, mud, and steel that Jaffar called "home."

"Bring them into the study room," hollered the doctor, "and tell one of the servants to bring in some tea and biscuits while you are at it."

"I'll bring them myself, Abbu," twittered the boy, whose voice echoed throughout the house. With his old, gnarled hand, the doctor took off his reading glasses. He was 65 years old, with a bald head covered by a white skullcap and a magnificently long, white beard.

The doctor heard Jumman's feet pattering towards the study. In no time the door was opened. There stood Jaffar looking self-conscious. Behind him was his wife in a black burka, her face hidden, except for a netted mesh covering her eyes through which she stared at the doctor. In her arms she held a newborn swaddled in a beige cloth, the third of Jaffar's offspring.

The doctor smiled gently at the infant.

"Come ... come, Jaffar," said the doctor, pointing with his fountain pen to the sofa near him. "Sit ... sit down and rest yourselves. It must have taken you a long time to come all the way from the Bandra Reclamation Slum to here. How did you arrive?"

"We came by train," answered Jaffar.

"Good ... good, now sit ... sit, I implore you, rest yourselves. My little fellow will get you some tea and biscuits."

"Don't go through the trouble, doctor sahib," whispered Jaffar's wife, as she sat ill at ease on the sofa alongside her husband. "We came so you may bless our newborn."

"Splendid, splendid, and come over here and let me see the child. No, no you sit, dear, I'll come to you."

The doctor raised his worn-out, bony body slowly from his cushioned chair and moved towards Jaffar's wife. He could hear his adopted son running to the kitchen upstairs with such force that it was making the whole house tremble. The old professor took the child from Jaffar's wife's hand and cradled the baby in his own, beaming down at the infant. After a lot of cooing, the doctor looked to Jaffar's wife.

"Is it a boy or a girl?"

"She is my third girl, doctor sahib," murmured Jaffar's wife. Jumman at that moment entered the study from another door, carrying an immaculate silver tray with two cups of tea and a silver bowl of biscuits and cookies. He placed the tray gently on a tea table in front of Jaffar and his wife. Then he ran out of the room before the old doctor could stop him.

"This boy of mine is like a speeding car, always running," he said, laughing, while he cradled the baby girl.

"One of these days he will break his neck. You should see the way he runs up the stairs. Ha! It makes me shiver."

The doctor then handed the squirming baby girl back to her mother and returned to his place at the study table. Jaffar looked hungrily at the goodies set before him. He had not had a decent meal for weeks, let alone foreign biscuits and cookies. However, he did not touch them.

The doctor and the couple sat in silence for a few minutes, disturbed only by the running of Jumman's feet in and out of the different rooms in the house. It was Jaffar who, with much hesitation, broke the silence.

"Dr. Sheikh, you taught me history in my municipal school twenty years ago and helped me in many ways after that, even after I had to leave school to earn a living for the family." Jaffar looked at the baby girl in his wife's arms wriggling like a puppy. "Dr. Sheikh, this is my third child . . . my third girl child. If I have to look after her, I'll be ruined. I am in no such position to get all three of my girls married and to pay their dowries. I earn only 9,000 rupees a month working as a helper at a secondhand bookstore. Where ... where is the money going to come from?" Jaffar squirmed on the doctor's sofa, tears forming in his red, sleepless eyes. "I'll go bankrupt doctor, I ... I need advice!"

The doctor stared fixedly at Jaffar and nodded his head. He then turned his attention towards Jaffar's wife.

"What do you have to say, madam?" the doctor asked. The woman in the burka looked at her husband who gave her a glare, which seemed to influence her answer.

"I want a boy, doctor sahib. I have enough daughters now. Selma the eldest, Maria the second, and now this little one . . ."

"What's her name?" asked the doctor in an almost strict tone, as if he were in one of his classes at the Mumbai University.

Jaffar answered him. "We, we thought it best not to name her – not to name her at all."

"Why?" asked the doctor.

Jaffar wiped his tears. "Well, if we could get someone to adopt her then at least—at least it will lessen our burden or—if you could . . ."

"You people are all the same," muttered the doctor in anger that stopped Jaffar in mid-sentence. "You people will never change. I expected much better from you, Jaffar. You were my star student. To hear YOU, a man with some education, talk about a girl as a burden! Aren't you both ashamed of your conduct?"

The pattering of Jumman's feet could now be heard downstairs. Dr. Rahim Muhammad Sheikh placed his fountain pen back on its stand. Turning to Jaffar he said, "Did you think that I would help you to get rid of the baby? Disgusting, Jaffar ... disgusting. Are you trying to say that girls can't go to school? That girls can't earn a living after a decent education? That girls can't earn for their families? WHAT IN THE WORLD ARE YOU TRYING TO SAY JAFFAR?"

The parents of the baby girl lowered their heads in shame like reprimanded schoolchildren. The doctor wiped the sweat from his forehead with a black handkerchief from his kurta pocket. The pattering of Jumman's feet continued.

The doctor then, without any ceremony, opened a drawer of his study table where he kept some cash. He picked up a bundle of five hundred rupees and placed it on the tea table next to the tray of tea and biscuits and cookies.

"Take that amount and save it for your girl's education. Since you are in dire straits, I can loan you more, but please never ever say a girl is a burden."

The doctor then got up from his seat in a huff and with his withered finger pointed to an old black-and-white photograph that hung on the wall to the right of Jaffar. It was the photograph of a young lady in a hijab and salwar kameez.

"Look at her ... look," admonished the doctor. "She was my mother, a doctor of political science, and was a member of the Indian National Congress Party during Gandhi's Civil Disobedience Movement. For her research on the evils of capitalism and her findings, Harvard University awarded her a medal. At that time, she was already married and pregnant with me in her womb. Look at her, Jaffar, look ... look!"

Jaffar stared at the woman in the photograph posing for the camera with her hands folded over her chest, her eyes still sparkling even after all these years.

The doctor returned to his seat, easing himself down on his cushioned chair. "Remember this, Jaffar ... girls do not bring dowries, they bring medals home, and you will see it happening in your home with this very child."

Dr. Rahim Muhammad Sheikh then called out for his adopted son Jumman to return to the study. The little boy slid into the room and sat upon his adopted father's lap. He frowned when he saw they had not touched the goodies on the table.

"Abbu, don't they like our chocolate cookies and tea?"

"Never mind that," said the old doctor in a kind voice. "I want you to do me and this couple in front of me a favor; I want you to name their baby. They have run out of names for baby girls, and so they have entrusted the naming of the girl upon you, my young man, so tell me, what do you want to call her?"

Jumman stared at the babe in the mother's arms tentatively for a few moments with his mouth twisted into a smirk.

"If she is a girl, and she looks like a pretty one, they should call her after great-great-grandmother who was a poet and whose portrait hangs upon the wall of the second guest room upstairs."

"Splendid idea, Jumman," replied the doctor happily. "And for that you deserve a chocolate cookie from the silver tray."

Jumman leaped from his adopted father's lap, picked a huge chocolate cookie from the tray and began to nibble on it. Jaffar sniffled a bit as he saw Jumman eating the cookie, thinking, *Oh, if only he were my son!* He then caught the boy by his tiny, slender waist and brought him closer to him. "So, Jumman, what is her name then?" Jaffar asked.

"Whose name?" mumbled Jumman concentrating on his chocolate cookie.

"Your great-great-grandmother's, the one who was a poet?"

"Oh, her!" exclaimed Jumman, finishing the cookie and licking his fingers. "Her name was ALI AMINA SHEIKH."

"You made a mistake there, Jumman," twittered Dr. Rahim Muhammad Sheikh. "You put her father's name first."

"Oops, sorry, sorry," said Jumman, climbing back upon his adopted father's lap. When he faced Jaffar, he corrected his mistake. "It's Amina Ali Sheikh, sorry for the mistake. I was concentrating on the cookie."

"Amina," murmured Jaffar, staring at the polished wooden floor.

*

When they were leaving, Jumman escorted them outside and helped them get a taxi, the fare for which the doctor had placed in Jaffar's wife's hands. Except for the chocolate cookie eaten by Jumman, the contents of the silver tray remained untouched. The tea in both the cups had grown cold. The bundle of five hundred rupees was left on the glass tea table. Dr. Rahim Muhammad Sheikh slowly climbed the stairs to the second guest room, which was next to the storage room where some items from Greek and Egyptian antiquity were stored. He opened the door and beamed. There above the bed hung a huge painting of Amina Ali Sheikh in a black burka with only her face exposed. She wore gray gloves and socks with bright brown sandals. In her hand, she held an open book, but she was not looking at the book. She was looking at the painter with an inquisitive expression on her fair face.

The doctor shook his head and sat on the bed facing the lady he had never known, except through stories from his grandmother and from the poetry books Amina Ali Sheikh had published, all in Urdu.

He remembered a verse of the woman's lyrical poems, which his grandmother used to sing to him when he was a baby:

The dust of the ages migrates into the pearl,
Around a pretty girl's neck to bejewel her with a tear.
Many a moon has crept up with the dusty beams,

Contrary and Contemplative are my thoughts
so they seem.

As he stared at the portrait, he recalled the little infant girl he had cradled in his arms just some moments ago. He wondered what she would be like when she grew up. Would she be anything like the woman in the painting towering over his fragile body? The doctor's grandmother once told him that Amina Ali Sheikh also was an accomplished musician. She wrote lyrical poems and then put a tune to them and played them on a violin, piano, or the sarangi. At the same time, she was a dutiful housewife and a splendid host to her guests. The doctor's grandmother told him that Amina Ali Sheikh had even played the violin solo at a concert in the then Calcutta Province of the British Government, stunning all the gora sahibs into silence. Her performance received thunderous applause and a call for an encore.

While the doctor mused over the past, Jumman returned home sweaty at the armpits from all the running he had done searching for a taxi for Jaffar's family. Jumman banged the teak wooden door shut and continued his ramblings about the house.

*

Khadijah wobbled around the room in her shanty with a scowl upon her face. Jaffar was seated on the muddy dung-caked floor cradling little Amina, while his wife fed Maria, the two-year-old, some mutton gosh that they had saved and had been eating for the past week. Selma sat next to her father, talking to herself and playing a game of nick-knack with her fingers and toes.

The old lady, who was getting irritated by the noise Selma made, screamed. "WILL YOU KNOCK IT OFF, YOU LAZY GIRL? Remember, a woman must never be seen and must never be heard."

Selma, not to be outdone, as it was occasionally her custom, retorted, "Well, grandmother, even you are a woman. Yet you make the most noise in our shanty."

"Fiendish wretch," exclaimed Khadijah as she pulled Selma by the hair until Jaffar intervened.

"Leave her alone," he cried, cradling the infant in his left hand and petting Selma's head where her hair had been pulled. "She is only a little girl."

Khadijah grunted aloud like a pig and slouched down on the muddy floor next to Jaffar's wife. "It's all well for your high-and-mighty teacher to think that girls are no burden. He is a rich man, after all. If he was so much an advocate of girls, why didn't he adopt a girl instead of a boy? Can anyone give me an answer?"

The silence in the room stung like a bee's bite.

"See," continued Khadijah, "no answer ... I will give you an answer. He basically wants to continue his family name, the Muhammadan Sheikhs of Gandhi's era. Ha!"

Jaffar's wife stopped feeding Maria and wiped the curry from the little girl's cheeks with the end of her dirty yellow sequined salwar kameez, her only salwar kameez.

Selma was paying close attention to what her grandmother was saying. She did not understand what "continue his family name" meant, and she certainly did not know who Gandhi was. However, to stay silent about things she didn't know was contrary to her inquisitive nature.

"Who is Gandhi, grandmother?" asked Selma.

"None of your concern!" blared Khadijah.

Jaffar was more affectionate than his mother. "Gandhi is the father of our nation, India," said Jaffar, and before Selma could ask what "father of our nation meant," he raised himself up from the muddy ground, put Amina in his wife's arms, and left the shanty to go to pray the namaaz in the mosque a few yards away from his home.

Selma continued her game of nick-knack with her fingers and toes.

Khadijah looked at the face of the newborn babe and then at her daughter-in-law. "She looks just like you," whispered Khadijah in a mellowed tone. Her daughter-in-law knew from past experience that in such a mood, she could get to have a few decent words with her mother-in-law.

The wife of Jaffar replied, "All my daughters look just like me."

"That's for sure," said Khadijah, "And they all have your characteristic dimples on both cheeks. It will raise the stakes for them when they are older to get married."

The wife of Jaffar gave a weak smile. She started rocking the baby in her arms to sleep. Of all her girls, the newborn seemed the calmest of the lot and cried very little.

Khadijah ruffled the silky light brown hair of the infant, making Maria sitting next to them giggle. To please Maria, the old lady ruffled the infant's hair again. The two-year-old squealed with delight and clapped her hands.

Khadijah then tickled Maria under her chin. Maria did not like this, so she ran to her elder sister. Khadijah laughed, and so did the wife of Jaffar.

"She is cute, that second girl of yours—cute but quirky," said Khadijah, crossing her legs, making herself comfortable on the muddy floor. "So, what name did that old doctor give the baby?"

"Amina," answered the wife of Jaffar.

"Amina," echoed Khadijah, looking upward at the muddy ceiling of the shanty. "I remember having a friend called Amina way back when I was about Maria's age. We lived in the same village, and both our fathers were butchers."

"What happened to her?" asked the wife of Jaffar. Khadijah's smile faded from her face, but she continued to look at the ceiling.

"I don't know," murmured Khadijah. "I think she was married off to a taxi driver in Calcutta or Surat. I have really no clue. She was nine when her mother dressed her up in her bridal finery and got her married. I still remember the dress. It was off-white with golden borders. I can't recall now whether it was a saree or a ghaghra, but she didn't look like a bride, just like a kid, a lamb, like the ones we slaughter during Bakri-Id."

Maria and Selma both ran out of the shanty. They heard the muezzin of the mosque calling the faithful to pray, but they continued to play a game of catch and cook. It was evening, and the people of the slums were returning to their huts or shanties. Maria slipped over some human excreta as she tried to catch Selma, who had by that time climbed into one of the MCGM dustbins, which was filled with plastics, paper, food, urine, and dead animals.

Khadijah, unaware of her grandchildren's activities, spat out some phlegm from her mouth at the doorstep of their shanty.

"So, are you going to send your girls to school?" she asked, wiping her mouth with the back of her left hand. Jaffar's wife looked down at the little baby Amina and remembered all the stalwart ladies in Dr. Rahim Muhammad Sheikh's photographs. She also recalled his words: *Girls do not bring dowries; they bring medals home.*

"Yes, I will, starting with Selma this year," replied the wife of Jaffar confidently.

Khadijah laughed. "It's your funeral, bahu. Then don't come running back to me saying that all your money is lost on pencils, pens, books, and slates for girls who have no future but to do the kitchen work in somebody else's house. Mark my words, bahu … mark my words."

The baby Amina gave a soft cry near her mother's bosom. The wife of Jaffar immediately got up gently from the ground and entered the inner room to breastfeed her baby. Khadijah rose unceremoniously from the floor and drew the shade of rags that separated the two tiny claustrophobic rooms in their shanty.

*

"Come inside, Tarabai, and seat yourself gently on the floor," said Khadijah in a pleasant voice, helping her guest, a woman around her daughter-in-law's age, to sit down on the floor of Jaffar's shanty. "May Khuda bless you immensely, neighbor, and may he gift your maternity with a male heir."

Tarabai was a Hindu neighbor of Khadijah. She lived a few blocks away from Khadijah's shanty in a mud hut near a gutter in the same slum, and she was with child.

Khadijah called out to Selma, who was outside the shanty playing hopscotch near a huge pile of garbage a week old. She ordered her to make some tea for the pregnant Tarabai. Selma abruptly stopped her game, entered the shanty, and crossed between the two ladies, going straight into the inner room.

Tarabai, who was dark and hefty, with a huge black bindi on her forehead, marveled at Khadijah.

"I have to admit, Khala, that you have really taught your girls how to maintain a house."

Khadijah chuckled. "They bloody well have no choice. After all, they are just girls."

"How are you keeping in health, Khala?"

"I'm always in the pink of health by the mercy of Khuda, the most compassionate," answered Khadijah. "I may not be praying five times a day, but I do all my duties as the eldest of this shanty in Khuda's name and, Khuda gavah hai (God is a witness), that I have done my best."

"That's wonderful," replied Tarabai. "That's really good, but Khala, I am worried."

"What about?"

"This . . . this baby," replied Tarabai hesitantly. "As you know, Khala, we are very poor. We live in a one-room mud-and-clay hut, and not so lavishly as you in this shanty."

Khadijah chuckled at the word *lavishly* but did not interrupt Tarabai.

"Well, Khala, this will be my first born. Suppose it is a — a girl. Then, it will be too much for us. The doctors at Holy Family Hospital refuse to let my husband and me know the sex of the child. If we knew, at least we could have had an abortion done."

"What, are you crazy?" exclaimed Khadijah. "The surgeon's fees would make you all more bankrupt than the girl will. Besides, why worry? You are young, strong, and hardworking. Even if the first is a girl, you can try for a boy later. Khuda is merciful to the poor, remember that."

Tarabai nodded her head in comprehension, but she wore a sad look on her face. Selma at that moment entered the room with two small glasses of tea and placed them on the muddy floor next to Tarabai and Khadijah. Selma then skipped out of the house to continue her game. Both the ladies sipped their tea. Tarabai moaned a few minutes after she had downed the contents of her glass.

"Whatever is the matter?" asked Khadijah, hoping Tarabai was not getting an ache too early in her pregnancy. "Are you getting some pain in your womb?"

"Oh, no ... no, Khala," said Tarabai, trying to hide her tears, "It ... it was the tea. Do you know that my husband and I, even though we both work, do not earn a sufficient wage to buy tea leaves for tea?" Tarabai dabbed her eyes with the end of her torn saree pleat. "Thank you, Khala, for giving me tea today."

"Don't be silly, dear," said Khadijah, holding one knee of Tarabai. "Come around anytime for tea. Come every day. My Selma may be only six and a half, but she makes tea as good as her mother. Bit of a snob and inquisitive as a CID officer."

Tarabai smiled and both the ladies hugged each other. After their embrace, and after Tarabai had dabbed away the last of her tears, Tarabai changed the topic of the conversation.

"By the way, Khala," she said, "how is the newborn?"

"Who? Amina?" smirked Khadijah, "She is doing fine, tamest of the lot, rarely cries and sleeps most of the time. Her mother has taken her out with the other one, Maria, to the dargah for blessings. When is your baby due?"

"In five months' time, during the winter."

*

In the New Year, Selma was sent off to school. Although she was old for the class, they placed her in the junior kindergarten, and though Khadijah disagreed most vehemently, they decided to put her into an English Medium School rather than a cheap BMC Marathi Medium School.

Maria soon followed as time went by. To make ends meet, the wife of Jaffar decided, with his consent, to become a saleswoman in a burka shop on Mohammad Ali Road near Dr. Rahim Muhammad Sheikh's home.

Due to the proximity to the doctor's house, the wife of Jaffar visited him quite often, mainly to hear the kind doctor illustrate the achievements of all the Muslim women in his family, whose black-and-white portraits hung upon the walls of his ancient home. When a year had passed, the wife of Jaffar had learned the names of these educated women and their achievements by heart.

Munira Ali Sheikh—poet, sculptor and painter

Bismillah Muhammad Ali Sheikh—lawyer

Nazneen Noor Sheikh—human rights activist and an advocate of widow remarriage

Pakeeza Noor Sheikh—poet and teacher

Zayn Ali Noor Sheikh—professor of English literature at the Mumbai University, a graduate from Harvard University

Tasneem Muhammad Sheikh—poet and painter, and lastly Amina Ali Sheikh—poet and musician

"One day all my daughters will become like these women," the wife of Jaffar said with a twinkle in her eye.

Along with their regular education, the wife of Jaffar requested a local maulvi to teach her girls how to read the Quran in Arabic. Selma was a fast learner. Maria was not that fast but was hardworking and industrious, so she was never far behind Selma.

By this time, Jaffar and his wife were earning about 12,000 rupees a month, and most of it was used to educate their girls.

Khadijah watched all the surrounding happenings with scorn, chewing betel leaves, and then behind her son's back, admonishing and abusing Selma and Maria for neglecting their household chores.

"Selma," once ordered Khadijah, "will you, for jannat's sake, lift your head from that schoolbook and go and make me some tea?"

Being the person she was, endowed now with superior intelligence, Selma replied to the shock of Khadijah, "Why don't you make it yourself? My teacher says that child labor is forbidden in India!"

"You vicious urchin covered in dung!" yelled Khadijah. "I'm going to trash your head!" After which she flung Selma's notebook out of the shanty and pulled her long ebony hair until the girl's cries echoed the sound of the muezzin calling all the faithful Muslims to pray:

Allah is Great

Allah is Great

I declare there is no other God but Allah

and Muhammad is the messenger of Allah

Come to pray, come to do good work

Come to pray, come to do good work

Since Jaffar still in his heart of hearts wished for a boy, he and his wife did not follow any family-planning policy. Therefore, by the time Selma was fourteen years old, the wife of Jaffar had given birth to two more girls and then, at last, a boy, but he was stillborn.

"You're cursed, bahu, you witch!" Khadijah screamed on the day of the stillborn child's funeral. "You are cursed with a womb only for good-for-nothing girls. Woe to my family. Khuda, why have you abandoned my family? You give a boy and take him away in an instant."

All the men, including Jaffar, with a disillusioned expression on his face, went off to bury the child in the Muslim Kabristan.

Khadijah was uncontrollable, beating her chest and sobbing so loudly that mucous started dripping down from her nose on to her raven black burka. The wife of Jaffar did not comfort her, and neither did she cry. She just sat on the muddy floor, holding her thin legs to her breast, beside Selma who sat staring at her grandmother's disgusting display of grief.

Standing inside the shanty were many Muslim women, along with the Hindu Tarabai, trying to calm Khadijah down.

Among them stood an eight-year-old girl, with light brown hair and immaculate fair skin. She was dressed in her school uniform, a white blouse with a white shirt and white sash along with a white hijab that was a bit too tight and too small to cover her full hair.

One of the women present took note of her, and asked Tarabai, "Oye Tarabai ... Tarabai, who was that pretty girl in the school uniform and light brown hair?"

"Her?" said Tarabai before she entered her hut. "That's Jaffar's third daughter, Amina. She is the one who plays the flute all the time and is as old as my Nirmala, just a bit older. She is a peculiar one, that she is, all said and done. Poor Khadijah, saddled with five granddaughters ... poor Khadijah Khala."

*

When Tarabai gave birth to Nirmala, who was dark skinned, thin, and weak, she and her husband Ramesh Acharya wanted to get rid of her in secret, so they dumped the baby Nirmala in a dustbin just after Tarabai was discharged from the hospital. The plan was to tell their slum-dwelling neighbors that the baby had died in child-birth.

However, they were found out by a group of rag sellers who had emptied the dustbin. With the help of an NGO, they managed to trace the parents of the baby girl. Tarabai was furious, but what could she do but accept her fate?

Nirmala grew up to be a very hardworking and bright child in studies but was abused physically and psychologically by both her parents, especially her mother.

The Acharyas tried for a boy and luck favored them. Nirmala became the sister of not one but three baby brothers, whom she tutored and cared for diligently under the strict supervision of her torturer Tarabai.

Nirmala would endure her suffering in silence, consoled only with the thought that one day she would become a doctor and continue her studies in the college of her dreams, St. Andrews College, Bandra.

One weekend during the school break in the heat of the scorching tropical sun, Nirmala squatted outside her hut giving her youngest brother Javed a bath near the gutter next to her poor hut. Taxies, buses, cars, and rickshaws passed along the road in front of Nirmala at the Bandra Reclamation Slum where she, Khadijah and the other poverty-stricken slum dwellers stayed. It was built on either side of the main road going towards the sea link. Nirmala coughed as the fumes from a truck heavily laden with grain passed her hut, emitting a lot of smoke. She tried to wave the fumes away with her wet soapy hand and continued to bathe Javed.

Khadijah, who sat on a charpoy chewing betel leaves watched Nirmala doing her job.

"Now that's what a girl should be doing," she said to the wife of Jaffar, who sat next to her on the charpoy with a lamb in her arms, feeding it some grass from a neighboring field. "Helping around the house and learning how to look after children, not being involved with books and studies and thoughts of collage."

"That's 'college,' mother-in-law," corrected the wife of Jaffar.

"College ... collage ... mollage, whatever it may be, it is not for girls... Not for girls!"

The wife of Jaffar did not respond. She had learned to turn a deaf ear to her mother-in-law and her rantings. As the wife of Jaffar picked up another blade of grass and coaxed the little lamb to eat it, she heard a flute playing in the distance.

"There we go again," grumbled Khadijah, her teeth red with betel juice. "It's that Amina again playing the flute like that Hindu God Lord Krishna, instead of doing her chores." Khadijah spat the betel juice on the road and wiped her filthy mouth with the end of her soiled black hijab. "She is the dumbest of the lot. At least Selma and Maria stand first in class—this third one of yours even hates your precious schoolbooks. All she does is play musical instruments, especially that blasted flute Jaffar got her for her birthday."

"She is a musical prodigy, mother-in-law," replied the wife of Jaffar. "Don't you realize that? Without instruction from a guru, she can play three musical instruments by ear: the flute, the mouth organ, and the pipe."

"Yes, and it's that blasted flute that irritates me the most," grunted Khadijah. "Who does Amina think she is, A.R. Rehman?"

"She is just trying to be herself, mother-in-law," said the wife of Jaffar, lifting herself from the charpoy and placing the lamb on the ground where it started to defecate. "Just give her a chance, and she too will do well in her studies."

Khadijah growled a curse as the wife of Jaffar, in her black burka, returned to their shanty to cook dinner. She then looked again towards Nirmala's mud clay hut; the girl had gone into the hut along with her brother. The old woman adjusted her hijab as she observed her neighborhood while the flute continued to play in the distance.

Piles of garbage taller than the huts and shanties in the area were everywhere. Some naked urchin boys defecated near grimy and germ-infested dustbins, which reeked with the smell of urine and excreta. Near one dustbin a man sold vegetables to an overwhelming number of customers, while near another dustbin a woman squatted on the ground selling paan, khadi shakar, and almonds. A group of young Muslim boys played a game of cricket in the middle of the road, disrupting traffic, while on her right a worker scrubbed a large vessel with ashes, which she knew would be sent to the local restaurant, the only restaurant in the Bandra Reclamation Slum called "Gharib Khana," or The Poor House. A gutter had overflowed to her left, creating a large pool of dirty black water. Two Muslim girls in black hijabs swam in that water, happiness showing all over their faces. Near the local mosque, some elderly gentlemen discussed something intently, while on top of a pile of wet garbage, some naked street urchin girls played upon the polluted pile, using it as a slide.

"Is this our life?" Khadijah said to no one in particular. The flute continued to play. If Khadijah had known better, she would have realized that the third girl child of Jaffar was playing the flute to the tune of Bankim Chandra's song for the nation "Vande Mataram . . . Vande Mataram!"

*

"Where is Amina, ammijaan?" asked Selma, peeping into the shanty. Her mother was feeding the youngest of the girls, named Feroza, while the fourth child, named Afsheen, was fast asleep on a dirty rag lost in her dreams.

"Not in here," answered her mother. "Check the garbage piles near the broken-down public urinal; she must be playing with Tarabai's daughter, Nirmala."

"Nope, checked that."

"Did you check under the bridge where the kolis sell their fish?"

"Yep, not there, either."

"Tarabai's hut?"

"Not there."

"Playing with the pariah dogs near Shantaram's shanty?"

"Not there, either."

"What exactly do you want her for?" the exasperated wife of Jaffar asked Selma as she rubbed the porridge smudges off the face of Feroza with the end of her hijab.

"There is a movie being shown at the Paradise Picture House about the life of the famous musician Mozart. It's in English. I thought she might be interested, being so musically inclined and all."

Outside the shanty, a boy in rags chased the chickens with a stick while his sisters ran after him to make him stop by screaming and squealing like mad cats during the mating season.

"Oh, great, is it Mozart?" beamed the wife of Jaffar. "Then we will all go, at least whoever you can find around here. Do you have money for the tickets?"

"Yep, it's in my purse," said Selma. "I'll go look for Amina and Maria, but please, ammijaan, don't take grandmother Khadijah along with us. She will not understand the language and will spoil the show, giving us a running commentary with each passing scene."

The wife of Jaffar laughed heartily. Seeing her mother laugh, Feroza gurgled a porridge-lipped smile. Her mother lifted her up and started to put a cute floral-colored hijab over Feroza's face. Selma ran out with the speed of a leopard, calling out to Maria.

In the end, however, Amina could not be found. Jaffar was stuck in traffic at Juhu, where he had taken Khadijah to see some cousins. Therefore, only the wife of Jaffar, Selma, Maria, Afsheen, and Feroza, all clad in hijabs, went for the movie at the Paradise Picture House. The wife of Jaffar informed him of their movie date via her secondhand Nokia cell phone, and he stated that she should not worry and take her time coming back to the shanty.

By the time it was 9:00 p.m., Jaffar and Khadijah returned to their shanty. When Jaffar opened the steel door, he saw his third daughter, Amina, fast asleep on the rags where Afsheen had slept in the afternoon, flute in hand and smelling strongly of cow dung.

Jaffar laughed, pointing his index finger at Amina. "No wonder they could not find her. The musician was playing her flute in the new milk and dairy farm come up near the fag end of the slum. By the smell of it, she must have even helped the ladies there to make dung cakes for fire."

"Pooh!" Khadijah exclaimed, pinching her nostrils shut with her fingers, "This girl was certainly a Hindu in her last birth, if the last birth theory is true; she loves cows like the pig his fodder. Eh! Girl!" said Khadijah, kicking her leg and waking her up. "Go and wash at the well in the fields. You smell like something the cat dragged in. Off with you now, get out!" Khadijah then wobbled her fat self into the kitchen to cook some mutton gosh, while Jaffar sat down at the place his daughter had just vacated. He grinned. The girl had taken the flute with her.

*

"It's 11:00 p.m., for heaven's sake!" screamed Khadijah, as she squatted down on the muddy floor of the shanty. "Where are they? This is no time for decent Muslim women to be out on the streets!"

Jaffar paced up and down the shanty, a worried expression on his aged face. It was not like his wife to remain out of the house so late, even if it was an evening show. Amina sat on her haunches, her white hijab was in the corner and her hair hung loose, falling in beautiful ringlets all the way down to her knees. She was cutting yam, the cheapest of all vegetables, for her sisters and mother, so that tomorrow they could eat it for breakfast and take it to school for lunch.

Jaffar had called his wife fourteen times but had received no reply. As the minute hand of his watch ticked on, Jaffar's heart began to beat anxiously in his throat.

Suddenly the occupants of Jaffar's shanty heard a noise from the streets. Jaffar brightened up.

"It must be them," he said, running outside to greet his wife and adorable girls. However, instead of them, he was shocked to find all the occupants of the slum running amuck. Chaos and confusion clouded their faces. Some were screaming into their cell phones, some running from shanty to shanty or hut to hut, others were gathering in the streets and blocking the traffic.

Jaffar ran towards Shantaram's shanty. Shantaram was the local electrician and matchmaker, and his shanty was just two paces away from Jaffar's poor dilapidated shanty. He was busy on his cell phone, literally screaming into it, while his workers mumbled to each other in a sort of escalating panic.

Jaffar caught hold of Shantaram's thin hand and shouted, "What's happened? WHAT'S HAPPENED?"

"Didn't you switch on your television? Bomb blasts ... Multiple bomb blasts all over the city."

"Where? Where?"

"On the streets, in hotels, in taxies, trains on the western line. One by one! Put your damn TV on and see!"

"Star News says six, but Zee News says eleven. Roads are blocked; people are running like crazy dogs, terror-stricken. It's ISIS supposedly." Then he put his phone back to his ear and shouted, "Hello! Hello!"

When Jaffar implored him to tell him more, Shantaram pointed towards his shanty where the television was tuned to the news channel on which the anchor Arnab Goswami declared that blasts were going off like Diwali fireworks all over the city of Mumbai.

One of the workers clad only in a dirty dhoti pointed at the television set propped upon an old stool in Shantaram's shanty.

"Look ... watch. It's terrible; they have even bombed theaters."

At that moment, a cold dead hand caught hold of Jaffar's heart and stopped it from beating.

"Theaters," he mumbled in a toneless voice.

"Yes ... yes, Jaffarbhai. Look ... look at the television."

Jaffar stooped to enter the small, overcrowded shanty made of bricks and steel with two floors to it. As he watched with terror on his face, he noted in his mind the places where the bomb blasts had taken place. Shantaram was right, bombs were exploding in taxies, on the road, in hotels, restaurants, bus depots, malls, and—theaters. Still, Jaffar hoped for the best. Maybe his wife and children were stuck in traffic. Maybe they were walking home. Maybe they were running ... panicking ... or ... or ...?

Arnab Goswami blared out the instructions for the masses to calm down, to refrain from causing pandemonium. But what did Arnab Goswami know of the pandemonium happening in the pit of Jaffar's stomach?

Riots between the Muslims and the Hindus had broken out at Vasai. A suicide bomber had blown up a market in Matunga, but none were worse than the number of theaters that had been bombed, killing hundreds of innocent people all over Mumbai.

Jaffar gritted his teeth and clenched his fist as if he were having a stroke. On the television, Arnab Goswami started calling out the names of the theaters that had been bombed between 8:30 p.m. and 11:00 p.m.

Roxy Theater—Charni Road

Eros Cinema—Churchgate

Albert Theater—Girgaum

Plaza Cinema—Dadar

Chitra Cinema—Dadar

Paradise Picture House—Mahim

Star City—Shivaji Park

Phoenix Mills Cinema—Kurla

Jaffar's tears chilled his already cold flesh as he read the name Paradise Picture House on the television screen. Paradise Picture House ... Paradise Picture House.

When he could not stand it any longer, Jaffar fainted into the arms of the worker who had spoken to him.

The worker tried to shake Jaffar awake while Shantaram continued to scream into his cell phone.

*

Amina sat quietly on the rags where her grandmother Khadijah had awakened her from sleep. She was wearing her school uniform, but not her hijab. She sat on her haunches, staring into infinity. Her wooden flute was by her side, but she did not touch it.

Chaos continued outside her shanty. Her grandmother had left her in charge while she and Jaffar went to the respective hospitals where the dead and the injured had been taken.

Amina's fair skin had grown paler and her lips were dry. A mosquito entered the shanty through the open door and buzzed above her head. It settled down in her hair, pricked its needle-like snout into her flesh and drank her blood. Amina felt the prick, but she did not drive the insect away, nor did she try to kill it. A string of boils started to form on the eight-year-old's head.

The stench of dried human excreta wafted its way into the shanty, but Amina did not close the door. The mosquito left after having its fill.

People passed her door, shouting and screaming curses, but nothing affected her. Shantaram, along with his workers, was directing the traffic. Some women of the Reclamation slums were providing biscuits and coffee to those stuck in the traffic. Amina wished to join them. From her open doorway, she could see her friend Nirmala along with her mother, Tarabai, providing small disposable cups of cold coffee to the people in taxis, buses, trucks, and cars stuck on the road due to the impenetrable traffic. Nirmala, in her trademark parrot green salwar kameez, kept to her mother's heels, but Amina, though willing in spirit, could not get up from the place where she was seated. She wanted to, but she couldn't.

In the silence of her shanty, Amina heard voices echoing in her mind. She heard her eldest sister, Selma, cracking a joke about the current political situation as she oiled Maria's long jet-black hair. Selma, with her wit and flamboyancy, wanted to become an IAS Officer. She had made her intention clear, despite taunts from her nemesis, Khadijah, their grandmother.

"I will study psychology and then take my exam and become an IAS Officer," Selma once said when she was in the eighth standard as she was getting her burka on.

"What is 'psychology'?" asked Khadijah vehemently.

Selma giggled.

"The study of human nature and mental activities, which I am afraid you do not possess, dear grandmother. Ha, ha, ha!"

Amina smiled weakly, recalling Khadijah's bewilderment, and Selma, bright and pretty Selma, oiling the demure Maria's hair, jet-black hair, Maria ... Maria!

Maria wanted to become a teacher at a school. She wanted to teach history and geography.

Jaffar was a bit in disagreement with her plans. "Why art subjects when you are so good in the sciences and mathematics, Maria?" he once asked her as he cradled the newborn Feroza in his arms. Maria did not react. She just chuckled to herself and continued to read a novel as she sat on her haunches next to her mother.

What was she reading that day? *Oliver Twist? Lolita? One Flew Over the Cuckoo's Nest? Hamlet? To Kill A Mockingbird?* Amina tried as hard as she could, but she couldn't remember the book ... Maria!

Suddenly the temperature in the shanty dropped and Amina felt a chill run up her spine. She drew her legs towards her, hugged them tight to her chest and rocked herself – backward – forward – backward – forward – backward – forward.

"TWO MORE DAUGHTERS!" Amina heard her grandmother Khadijah yell in the recesses of her memory when on one Sunday morning the wife of Jaffar brought Afsheen home for the first time. "You two are mad, completely mad! How are we going to pay their dowries? How will we ever be able to afford to get them married? Together you earn 12,000 rupees a month, only 12,000 a month!"

"Oh, shut up, grandmother," snapped Selma, as she continued to peer into her notebook. "Some of us here are trying to study."

"Study ... study ... study," mimicked Khadijah, "that's all you all do! Who is going to do the chores? Your mother has brainwashed you all because of that blasted professor from Mohammad Ali Road. You've all got airs!"

"We are not hot air balloons, grandmother," said Selma. "Stop saying we got airs, airs, airs. Just wait till we all start working and earning for the family. Then you will see the money coming in. Till then, stop irritating us and chewing betel leaves; you remind me of a cow chewing its cud!"

That time the whole family laughed, except Khadijah.

Amina sniffled. Unlike her sisters Selma was so bold and so strong. Was she really already dead at age 14 years two months and seven days?

"Ammijaan, Amina does not study with Maria and me," Amina heard Selma's voice in the silence of the poor shanty. "All she does is play her musical instruments. Can't you discipline her, ammijaan?"

The wife of Jaffar would turn a head towards Selma and say, "You watch, gudiya, my Amina may not be sharp in studies, but she can play music like an ustad. Dekhna, she is a prodigy, a musical prodigy. Dr. Rahim Muhammad Sheikh says that one day he will help me to enroll my Amina into a musical academy somewhere in Bandra. Just be patient, Selma. Amina will also bring laurels to the family."

"Whatever!" Selma would mumble, getting back to the mathematical equations her schoolteacher had given her for homework. Then Amina would sneak over and massage Selma's tired feet and calves, and she would smile. How Amina loved that dimpled smile!

Feroza and Afsheen were the angels of the family. They were never corrected and were doted upon by the wife of Jaffar.

"You watch and see, Selma," the wife of Jaffar once said. "My Feroza will become a fashion designer and my Afsheen a doctor, just like Tarabai's daughter. Nirmala wants to become a doctor when she grows up." Then she tickled Afsheen under her arms to make her giggle with glee. "See how she laughs, my tiny Afsheen!"

The words echoed in Amina's head: *My tiny Afsheen – Afsheen – bomb blast – Paradise Picture House – ammijaan – ammijaan!*

Nirmala timidly entered Jaffar's shanty and found her friend on the floor, rocking back and forth upon some rags. She went towards Amina and hugged her tightly.

"Everything is going to be okay, Amina," Nirmala said gently. "Everything is going to be okay."

*

The next morning, five bodies in Jaffar's shanty lay wrapped in the pristine white cloth of the dead before they would be placed in their graves. Jaffar sobbed, wailed, and screamed. He was inconsolable. He tore his kurta, pulled his hair as he ranted on and on, while Ramesh Acharya, the father of Nirmala, and Shantaram held him before he could do any more harm.

"This is not fair. THIS IS NOT FAIR!" screeched Jaffar, his face red like a beetroot. "Why my family, Allah, why my family? They were sinless; they just wanted to see a movie. Allah, why? Why? Why?"

Khadijah sat on her haunches, holding Amina close to her. Dr. Rahim Muhammad Sheikh stood next to them in a pristine white sherwani above a pair of well-ironed white pants. He stood motionless as if in a daze, staring at the bodies placed in a row like a mute spectator who had nothing to do with the family. Jaffar, however, continued to cry.

"People bury the bodies of their dead, but look at me. I don't even have the bodies of my youngest children—just their faces and some parts of their stomach and intestines—my Selma—no head. I had to recognize her by her glass bangles and anklets. Allah, why? Why? Why?"

At the mention of Selma, Khadijah began to cry. Amina put her arms around her grandmother, but Khadijah continued to weep.

"Shantaramji," Jaffar cried out, "Shantaramji, we Muslims wash the bodies of our dead before we bury them, but my Maria was only a pile of hair, flesh, blood, and ashes kept on a table above my headless Selma in Hinduja Hospital. I recognized her because of the remains of the book she was reading. Do you know what she was reading? Bloody hell, she was reading *Gitanjali* by Rabindranath Tagore, her favorite author. Hair, flesh, blood, and ashes. I couldn't even hold her together. ... Ya Allah!"

The mourners, who until then had stood like statues, began to weep along with Jaffar. Amina bit her lip so hard she drew blood. Khadijah wailed. In her torn dark blue saree, Tarabai wiped a tear that had rolled down her dark cheek. Nirmala stood next to her, pale and silent.

Dr. Rahim Muhammad Sheikh walked toward the inconsolable Jaffar, whose black kurta was in tatters, nose streaming with snot, and arms lifted toward the heaven.

"Jaffar, control yourself. Get a hold of yourself!" The doctor, who was at this point, frail and over seventy, placed his hand on Jaffar's shoulder. Jaffar threw the doctor's hand away in rage. "You ...You put it into our heads to educate our girls. YOU BLOODY SERPENT! They wouldn't have gone for that English movie was it not for you. Can you bring back the dead, doctor? Ya Allah, the least the hospital people could have done was to put a blanket over the dead body of my Rahat ... my Rahat, my sweet Rahat!"

Hearing the name Rahat, Nirmala got a bit confused. She nudged her mother and innocently asked her who this Rahat was.

"Idiotic little girl," growled Tarabai under her breath, "Rahat was the name of Amina's mother."

Nirmala was shocked to hear it. *Such a pretty name,* she thought to herself, but she never in the wildest of her dreams imagined the mangled body in a white cloth to be Amina's mother. Strange enough, the woman had always been known as the "wife of Jaffar." She seemed to have had no identity of her own, let alone a name! *Rahat.* What a pretty name, Amina's mother's name, a woman who wished to give her daughters an identity, now gone forever.

"Ya Allah!" wailed Jaffar, beating his chest as Ramesh Acharya and Shantaram tried to control him from harming himself.

The doctor, however, took off his spectacles with his old dried up and gnarled hands. He looked at the dead bodies and began to sing a couplet he had read from the works of his great-great-grandmother Amina Ali Sheikh:

Our destinies have come apart in haste,
Only Allah knows which place that you have
returned to;
I moan to tears, and I sigh in sobs,
Only my God can support me now because you have
gone.
Your memory in my soul will I keep,
No more with love shall I call out to your heart;
For you have traveled farther away,
My Allah will guide you on his way to the
tomb of silence.

Amina cried bitterly. She left Khadijah and ran to the motionless body of her mother and hugged her. Nirmala mutely stared while Tarabai swallowed her sob and dabbed her eyes with the end of her old saree. The doctor continued to sing:

I have lost my voice to call you from the grave,

When did I arise from my sleep and when did you
go to your rest?
I will die if I'm separated from your bosom
in any way,
I have lost my voice to call you from the grave.

*

It was a year after the serial bomb blasts that Tarabai
sat on a charpoy overlooking the grazing fields. Next to
her sat Khadijah, with her needlework, chewing betel
leaves. Her nails were filled with dirt and black with
grime. Tarabai observed the sheep and goats grazing on
the fields and heard the sound of a flute. Amina's flute.

"Poor girl," murmured Tarabai. "All her sisters are no
more; her mother is no more. What does she do when she
is not at school, Khala?"

"She obliges me by doing her assigned chores," answered Khadijah, not looking up from her needlework.
"And tries to study at night when she is not playing her
flute, pipe, or mouth organ. Dr. Rahim Muhammad
Sheikh wanted to gift her a piano, but I stopped him.
There is no place for us to sit in our shanty with painted
green walls—and he wanted to bring in a piano! Can you
believe it, Tarabai?"

The needle pricked Khadijah's thumb in the process of
a tricky stitch. "Ever since the death of my Rahat and her
daughters, my son has given up all hopes to educate and
get a job for this third girl who remained behind. She is

weird and too exotic looking. Now, if only my Selma would have been alive instead of this nincompoop, maybe we would be in high spirits now."

"What do you mean, Khala?" asked Tarabai.

Khadijah cut a part of the white string with her teeth. "My son, Jaffar, has grown silent. Amina's music reminds him of his dead daughters, so she can't play her musical instruments in the house. I broached the subject, asking Jaffar whether he would like to marry again, on your advice last week."

"Well, what did he say?" asked Tarabai.

The old woman sighed and pricked her finger again with the sharp needle. "He won't. He can't forget Rahat or his children, especially the little ones, Feroza and Afsheen. They were such angels. Complete farishtas as it is given in the Koran; they were so beautiful."

"Your Amina is beautiful also," interrupted Tarabai, "with her light brown hair and eyes. Now look at my Nirmala, so hopeless to look at. Darker skin than me, thin, and stinking of garbage and urine. She has no sense of hygiene at all! And her hair is so thin and limp. I bet because of her bad looks we will have to pay a heavy dowry. But Lord Vishnu is merciful. I've got three sons to support me in my old age."

"Aha, we'll see about that," chuckled Khadijah. "Remember, a son is a son till he gets a wife, while a daughter is a daughter all her life!"

Tarabai stared in amazement at Khadijah.

"Where did you get that quote from, Khala?"

Khadijah sniffed as she continued to stitch. "Selma, during one of her taunting sessions, read it from some book of hers, or was it Maria's book? Can't remember now. I've become too old and too weak to remember all of that now."

Suddenly a commotion occurred a few paces away. The flute had stopped playing. Little urchin boys, some completely naked, others dressed in dirty singlets, giggled with excitement. Nirmala, who was now nine years old, ran towards her mother, panting breathlessly.

"Ma ... Ma ... it's Amina ... Amina!"

Khadijah's heart skipped a beat. She put her knitting aside and grabbed Nirmala by her shoulder. "Now what has that girl done?"

Nirmala squirmed in Khadijah's grasp.

"It's ... it's a bit hard to explain. Amina has hurt herself very badly. *Very, very* badly. The urchin boys are making fun of her."

"Where is she?" asked Khadijah, panic-stricken.

"She is there." Nirmala pointed to a huge pile of garbage in front of a basket maker's shop. "She is hurt very badly. Come and see for yourselves."

The two women, along with Nirmala, ran toward the stinking pile of garbage. When they reached it, the sight they saw embarrassed them no end.

Amina, as was her custom, had been sitting on top of the pile of garbage and playing her flute. And now that whole area, and the part of the garbage pile Amina had slid down, was drenched in bright red blood.

"Shame, shame," giggled all the street urchins. Tarabai and Khadijah stood aghast. Below the garbage pile stood Amina in her school uniform and tight white hijab. Her flute hung limply in her hand while the back portion of her skirt was drenched in blood. Blood was also dripping down her inner thighs and her calves toward the filthy ground.

"See," Nirmala said, weakly, "I told you she was wounded."

"Foolish girl!" exclaimed Tarabai, hitting Nirmala on the head. "Can't you be more knowledgeable about things? The girl has got her period for the first time. We will need to wash her. Khala, don't worry. I'll handle this."

Tarabai grabbed Amina and Nirmala's hands and drew them away from the street into her tiny hut. Khadijah stood rooted at the place, completely stupefied as she stared at Amina's blood on the pile of garbage.

But she is only nine years old! The old woman thought. She then ran back to her shanty in complete embarrassment. The period would last for at least four days. Till then Amina would not be able to enter the kitchen. Khadijah would have to do the cooking for the three of them.

"Ya Khuda, musibat aur musibat, is that all you wish to do with us?" Khadijah mumbled as she wobbled her way into her shanty.

At night, while Khadijah, Jaffar, and Amina were eating their dhal and rice with chicken legs, Jaffar told Amina in a detached tone of voice, "Starting tomorrow you will not wear your old white hijab or your old school dress to school. You will wear a proper beige robe, which Selma used to wear, and a proper white hijab with pants, which Maria used to wear. I will give your teacher a letter explaining everything. Until the end of your period you will not enter the kitchen nor cook for us, do you hear?"

Amina nodded solemnly.

After dinner, Jaffar went out in the dark for a walk. It was an excuse to allow Khadijah to teach Amina how to use a tampon.

"And don't go on changing your pad through the course of the day; keep it on for a whole day and then use a rag cloth at night. We don't have enough money to spend on your period."

Jaffar returned home after two hours and went to sleep immediately. Amina fiddled with her mouth organ, practicing a Bollywood song she had heard on Shantaram's radio. Khadijah listened to the sensuous music played by her granddaughter as she steamed up some rice to feed a vagabond dog whom the old lady had befriended after the deaths of her daughter-in-law and granddaughters.

Amina's song echoed in the dark of the night all the way to Nirmala's impoverished hut where the girl sat outside on the threshold reading *David Copperfield* by Charles Dickens.

*

After the death of her mother and sisters, Amina grew more attached to her music and her best friend, Nirmala. They could often be found chasing chickens, playing hopscotch near the foul unmaintained garbage bins, accidentally pricking their heels with shards of broken glass—the remains of liquor bottles, which were consumed on a regular basis by the Bandra Reclamation Slums inhabitants, a temporary cure for aching empty stomachs.

Nirmala would often coax Amina to dig into the garbage bins reeking with the smell of urine to collect invaluable treasures. Though the petite Amina found this act disgusting at first, she dug into the garbage bins to please Nirmala. The two girls collected bottle tops, stamps, envelopes, discarded rags, discarded shoes, shoelaces, rag dolls, syringes left by slum drug addicts, and much more.

As the years passed, Amina grew demure and contemplative. By the time she was thirteen, she had taken over the household work and cooked food for her grandmother and father, unless it was the time for her period. Then the menopausal Khadijah would cook mutton gosh and serve it to the inmates of the shanty.

"Amina," Nirmala would often call out to her as she peeped into the shanty. "Oye, Amina, let's go out to play. I've just finished my chores for the day."

In answer, Amina would shake her head sadly as she kneaded the dough for making chapattis in the same aluminum tray that Selma once used. Nirmala always understood and went on her way.

Dr. Rahim Muhammad Sheikh made frequent visits to Jaffar's home. He would sit on the muddy floor, and Amina would give him tandoori chicken to eat. She then entertained the doctor by playing on her flute or pipe to the tune of a Christian hymn that she had heard at school, or to the tune of a Bollywood song.

"I implore you, Jaffar," begged the doctor holding Amina's father by the shoulders, "send this girl to a music academy and let her shine. She is unbelievably talented. She could one day give a concert performance."

Jaffar gazed into the doctor's eyes, which had turned yellow over the years, before looking at the picture of the Kaaba on his steel wall. He remained silent, allowing the doctor to describe the opportunities that Amina would come by if she trained at a music academy.

"She is a prodigy, Jaffar, a musical prodigy," the good doctor said. "She will bring laurels to your family."

"I have no family left," Jaffar stated in an emotionless voice, eyes fixed on the image of the Kaaba.

"Well, then," said the doctor in a frustrated voice, "what do you plan to do with her?"

At last Jaffar turned towards his teacher and answered him candidly. "I'll allow her to study till the tenth grade and then get her married off so that my burden shall be less."

"How dare you call your only remaining daughter a burden!" exclaimed the fragile doctor, whose ear-shattering coughs indicated two very sick lungs. Jaffar patted the doctor's thin back and motioned Amina, who was sitting in the room, to get a mug of water for the doctor. After a few gulps, the cough subsided, and the doctor found his voice again.

"Look, Jaffar, I'm an old man now. I ... I won't live much longer. I have good connections with the Furtado Music Academy who, with my letter of sanction, will teach your Amina for free. Please Jaffar, let her join Furtado's Academy. Answer me ... answer me now. ... You will send her, won't you?"

Jaffar looked away from the doctor and gazed at Amina. She stood in a jet-black robe and white hijab, her eyes were lowered to the muddy ground, no smile upon her face. Jaffar at that moment wondered what had become of the dimpled smile of his daughter. In its place dwelled a thin line, which supposedly was her mouth.

Dimples ... Rahat ... All his daughters had Rahat's dimples ... dimples ... Rahat, sweet Rahat.

"I'm sorry, doctor, but, I can't. I won't send Amina to the academy. Her place is in the kitchen, and after she finishes school, marriage."

The doctor scrutinized Jaffar's face skeptically.

"Do you know, Jaffar, that the legal age for a girl to get married in India is eighteen years of age?"

"Yes, I know that, doctor."

"Well, then why after the tenth grade? She ... the child will only be sixteen by then. At least let her do her twelfth grade—"

Jaffar raised his left hand, pausing the doctor mid-sentence. The doctor's wrinkles went slack. He had lost the battle. Amina shed silent tears as Jaffar led the aged Dr. Rahim Muhammad Sheikh out of the shanty. Before he left, Jaffar turned back towards Amina. "I'm going to get the doctor a taxi to go back to Mohammad Ali Road. While I'm gone, get on with cooking some chapattis for your grandmother."

Amina, red-eyed, nodded slowly and returned to the kitchen, while her father closed the door of the shanty.

*

One night, Amina was doing some needlework when she heard a scream followed by a girl yelling.

"Let go ... let go ... let go!"

At the sound, Jaffar woke from his sleep and stared at the clock hung on a nail above him, as did Khadijah. It was 10:35 p.m., hot and humid. Who could be screaming at this time of the night?

"What is it? Who is screaming?" grumbled Khadijah, pulling her dirty salwar dupatta over her head.

"That scream sounds like Nirmala, doesn't it, Amina?" Jaffar said with a worried expression on his face.

Before Jaffar could get up from his spot on the muddy floor, Amina dropped her needlework, put on the black hijab that once belonged to Maria, and dashed out of the house towards Tarabai's hut.

"Well," shouted Khadijah to her son, "what are you waiting for, Christmas? Go on and find out what's wrong. ... Go, go, go!"

Jaffar pulled on a brown kurta and dashed out of the shanty towards Tarabai's hut, which was built near the gutter. A crowd had gathered around a nearby street-light. Jaffar pushed his way through the crowd. What he saw froze him in place.

Nirmala's foot had been bitten by a huge bandicoot that tore chunks of her flesh and refused to let go, however much the girl shook her bleeding leg. Amina dropped to the wet, muddy ground and hugged Nirmala close to her chest. Jaffar frantically looked around for something to strike the animal.

"Amina!" shouted Jaffar. "Hand me that piece of broken glass near you. Quick girl, quick!"

Amina saw the glass and threw it to her father, who caught it at once. Tarabai and Ramesh Acharya, her husband, were staring stupefied with the rest of the crowd, while the bandicoot continued to chew on Nirmala.

Jaffar moved with haste. But Ramesh Acharya was quicker. He found a long, blade-like piece of glass at the side of the road and stabbed the filthy bandicoot with the pointed end. The animal's fur quickly became bloody and soon the giant rat fell on its side, dead.

Jaffar looked up at one of the slum dwellers. "Come on, get a rickshaw ready. The girl will have to be taken to the hospital immediately. Get some rags to stop the blood, and Tarabai ... Tarabai ... Hey, Tarabai, what are you doing?"

To the shock of Jaffar, Tarabai had taken off one of her slippers and began to beat Nirmala. Amina cradled her best friend in her arms, imploring her mother to stop, and in turn received some blows.

"You witch!" screeched Tarabai. "Now because of you, we will have to shell out money for a doctor. Where is that money going to come from? What was the need to sit out here under the streetlight, miserable wretch of a girl?"

Ramesh Acharya shouted, "Hit her, Tarabai. Hit her harder. She thinks that by studying under streetlights in the dead of night she will become a doctor. Hit her, Tarabai. Hit her!"

"Stop it, you two!" Jaffar stepped up and knocked the slipper out of Tarabai's hand. "She is bleeding profusely. She needs to be taken to the hospital. Where is that rickshaw now? Amina, hold on to her. She's shivering."

*

After the rickshaw took Nirmala away and Jaffar and Amina returned to their shanty out of breath, Khadijah wanted to know what happened. "Those screams were ear-shattering as if someone were being strangled."

"It was Nirmala," answered Jaffar, as he lowered himself to the muddy floor. "A bandicoot bit her outside her hut, where she was sitting under a streetlight."

Amina changed her robe and went into the next room to wash Nirmala's blood off her hands. Khadijah snorted. "What in the hell's name was she doing under that streetlight in the middle of the night?"

"Apparently studying," Jaffar said.

"Can't she study in her hut?"

"The television disturbs her, and they don't put it off so that she can read her novels and study in peace. So, she goes out and sits under the streetlight."

"Who has taken her to the doctors?"

"Shantaram got a rickshaw ready. Both Tarabai and Ramesh Acharya have gone with her. Amina has been told to take care of the little boys in the hut till they return. Amina, hey, Amina!" Jaffar called aloud. "Wash your hands quickly and run to Tarabai's hut. Off with you now, girl."

Amina emerged from the inner room, her hands wet. She opened the door of the shanty and ran outside. Khadijah adjusted her dupatta to cover her forehead before she said, "I bet Tarabai must have beaten her to death."

"Not to death, thanks to Amina and me," answered Jaffar sarcastically, "but beat her, she did—with her slipper."

"She deserved it."

"No, she did not, ammi. She wants to stand first in class and later on become a—"

"Ha, ha, ha," Khadijah cackled like a witch, interrupting Jaffar mid-sentence. "You think Tarabai, who dumped this girl in the dustbin less than a week after her birth, will shell out money to make her a doctor? No chance of that happening in this lifetime, certainly, if re-incarnation theories are true."

Jaffar remained silent, bending his head low. Khadijah raised her overweight self up and wobbled into the inner room.

"Amina has left a lot of blood all over the sink, stupid girl," said Khadijah, shaking her head from side to side. "When will she ever learn to be tidy? What will her in-laws say about her untidiness and her silly music?"

Khadijah tottered into the room where Jaffar was seated. She scratched her waist and then opened a tiny wooden cupboard's drawer, pulling out 500 rupees. Jaffar pretended to ignore that the tiny cupboard once was the study table of his eldest daughter Selma, but he was not doing a great job at it.

Khadijah thrust the money into Jaffar's hands.

"Tarabai is my good friend. It's the middle of April, and she will not have the money for hospital expenses.

Take the money to her right now. It is the least I can do for her, for I, too, have been saddled with a useless girl."

Jaffar opened his mouth to protest, but the sight of the tiny wooden cupboard shut him up like a clam. He took the money, counted it, and then left the shanty. Khadijah sighed as she shut the door of the shanty and then entered the inner room to clear the blood spots from the sink.

*

"Come in, Shantaramji," said Khadijah, motioning the thin bespectacled man with a jhola to enter and sit down on the muddy floor of her shanty. "So ... have you got anything worthwhile for me?"

The all-obliging Shantaram nodded. He put his hand into his jhola and brought out some photographs of young Muslim men. He placed them on the floor next to Khadijah. The old woman picked up one photograph and then another.

"Aha," she said with her eyebrows raised and a grin across her face. "You truly are the best matchmaker of Bandra, Shantaramji. What handsome young Muslim men you have carefully picked for my Amina to marry."

"All in a day's work, Khala," said Shantaram, adjusting his spectacles. "All are as per your wishes. None of them is a graduate, but all earn at least 13,000 rupees a month. Some have not even passed their matriculation examination but have businesses of their own at the Dharavi slum."

"Nah, nah, Shantaramji!" exclaimed Khadijah in response. "I'm not sending Amina to Dharavi whether the boy has a business there or not. That Tarabai's Nirmala has already got a proposal from Dharavi."

"Yes, yes. The boy's name is Dheeraj Manoharan," nodded Shantaram in affirmation, displaying his shining white teeth. "I brought the proposal and set them up. Ask Tarabai, when she comes to have tea at your place, whether or not we sat for an entire afternoon breaking our heads over each proposal until she was satisfied. Nirmala will be very happy, very happy!"

"I hope so," mumbled Khadijah, staring at each photograph minutely. "Her life here has been hell. She's been constantly, physically and psychologically, abused by her family."

"Wah, Khala," said Shantaram, his left hand raised towards the ceiling, "you are learning new English words nowadays. *Psychologically!* Who taught you this word, Khala?"

Khadijah's eyes welled up with tears as she recalled Selma taunting her, using the word as Khadijah tried to admonish her. Shantaram's smile disappeared and a worried look came over his face.

"Have I said something wrong, Khala?"

"Nah, nah, nothing, Shantaramji," Khadijah said, drying her eyes with the end of her black hijab. "I just ... I just remembered my Selma. Do you realize, Shantaramji, it's been eight years since those terrible bomb blasts took place? By the eleventh of this month, it will be eight years."

Shantaram smiled and frowned, both at the same time, as the elderly Khadijah sighed deeply.

"Well," she continued, "at least they were only girls so their deaths were not such a great loss to our family. Though I miss my dear Rahat like crazy sometimes – and sometimes even that Selma, although she had a sharp tongue."

Shantaram squirmed in place, eager to start the business of choosing a boy for Amina. Sensing his unease, Khadijah wiped the last of her tears with the back of her right hand and again started to scrutinize the photographs.

At the same time, Jaffar was busy at work at the secondhand bookstall. As he dusted the books with an old rag, he pondered over what must be going on in his house. His mother had informed him that Shantaram was arriving that day with proposals for Amina. She had just finished her tenth-grade board exams and had turned sixteen years old.

As Jaffar returned each book to its appropriate place on the shelves, he remembered with fondness his second daughter, Maria, who loved to read. He remembered how she could read a four hundred–page novel in just one night's time, and then return the book to her school library and get another one in its place, and read that book equally fast.

Jaffar then began to arrange the poetry books. As he expected, his hands fell upon Rabindranath Tagore's poetry collection *Gitanjali*— the last book Maria would read before—a bundle of hair, intestines, blood, and ashes. He placed the poetry book back on the shelf gingerly as if he were carrying a baby for the first time.

"Hey, Jaffarbhai!" called the owner of the secondhand bookstall. "Get me a glass of coffee, will you, and be a bit quick with the dusting."

"Yes ... yes, sir," stammered Jaffar, whizzing his way into another room to make the coffee.

Khadijah, at this time, was busy in a feisty conversation with Shantaram about the proposals.

"Hmm, this one looks a bit old, Shantaram."

"Just forty-three years of age, Khala, with a good business but no education."

"Nah, he won't do," declared Khadijah, giving the photograph back to Shantaram. "He looks old enough to be Amina's father. Does he like music? For that girl of ours will not give up playing her blasted musical instruments even at her in-laws. She has made that very clear, and I wish to humor her for her dead mother's sake."

"Absolutely, absolutely," said Shantaram, replacing the photograph in his jhola. "Take a look at the others, Khala, especially this one." He pointed to a photograph somewhere in the middle. "This boy... er, man is forty years old, passed his matriculation, and works for a private trading firm and, as per your wishes, he earns exactly 13,000 rupees per month."

"Yuck!" exclaimed Khadijah in disgust, flinging away the photograph. "He is dark as ebony and has a rattish look about him. Show me someone good-looking, please, Shantaramji. I don't want my great-grandchildren to have ratty black faces. Show me someone as fair as Amina."

Shantaram placed the photograph back into his jhola. He then adjusted his glasses again and began to think. Khadijah did not interrupt his thoughts and scratched her red henna-dyed hair. Shantaram put his hands into his jhola and searched it frantically. Khadijah began to twirl the cheap silver nose ring pierced in her left earlobe, a parting gift from her late husband. Five minutes later, he smiled, fished out a photograph and placed it in front of Khadijah on the muddy floor.

"Sorry for the delay, Khala, but as you can see for yourself, it was worth the search. His name is Iqbal Muhammad Merchant. He is a Sunni Muslim, just like you all, thirty-one years old or maybe even thirty-two and ... and if you see," Shantaram pointed to the photograph with his right index finger, "he is as good-looking as a Greek God, muscles, a fair complexion, and dark brown hair. However, he only earns 9,000 rupees per month. You wanted someone who would earn 13,000 rupees. Therefore I did not show you the photograph at first. See ... see if you are pleased with him."

Khadijah picked up the photograph of Iqbal Muhammad Merchant and smiled to herself. Indeed, he was very handsome.

"Shantaramji," said Khadijah, still admiring the photograph. "Tell me more about this boy . . . er man."

"Very nice boy . . . er man," replied Shantaram with a lot of enthusiasm, as if he were in his electrical shop selling a tube light to one of his customers. "Good family values, is the only child of the family, lives alone with his elderly mother, prays five times a day, and has his own business."

"What business?" asked Khadijah.

"Er... let me check," replied the eager Shantaram, taking the photograph from Khadijah's hand. He turned the photograph and squinted to read the notes he had written in Marathi, his native tongue, behind the photograph. As his vision adjusted to the small handwriting, he read aloud in Hindi for the illiterate Khadijah, who had again begun to scratch her hair.

"Sells ladies' nightgowns at Bhendi Bazaar on the streets ... er, has not been educated, but can speak English, Hindi, and Marathi very fluently. Wants a girl who has good family values and is below twenty years of age."

Khadijah nodded her head in delightful comprehension.

"Not bad, Shantaramji ... not bad at all. My great-grandchildren will look very pretty if my Amina marries this boy, er ... man. Does he like music?"

"It's not mentioned here," declared Shantaram, "but I could find out for you, if you are interested and with Amina bacchi's consent . . ."

"No need for her consent," replied Khadijah roughly. "She will marry whoever we choose. If we go by what she wants, we will go bankrupt. Just yesterday she whispered to me that she would like to marry a musician—bah!" Khadijah said with a growl. "This one never had any sense. Say no more, Shantaramji. I like this Iqbal Muhammad Merchant. Do what is needed so that in six months' time they are married off. Er ... has he asked for any dowry?"

"It's not mentioned here, Khala," said Shantaram, "but if I remember correctly, Iqbal's mother did not want a dowry, but Khala . . ."

"Excellent!" interrupted Khadijah. "Then it is settled. Who wants to spend money on this girl, anyway? Good-for-nothing musical daydreamer, that's what she is. The quicker she leaves the house, the better for all of us and her dead mother's soul, my Rahat."

"Yes, yes, Khala," said Shantaram with a smirk that was too obvious not to notice. "But you have forgotten something."

"What?"

"Age, Khala, age. Our Amina has just turned sixteen, and the legal age for a girl to get married in India is eighteen, so ... maybe I can tell Iqbal to wait for two years if ..."

"No *ifs* and no *buts*," said Khadijah in a commanding tone of voice that made the matchmaker shudder. "We will say Amina is eighteen years old. Lucky for us we have never divulged her age to anyone."

"Tarabai knows Amina is sixteen," said Shantaram, "as well as her family. She is, after all, five months older than our Nirmala bacchi."

"So what?" scowled Khadijah. "Nazira's granddaughter got married recently, and she was seventeen years of age and three months. Munira's daughter also got married to a man three times her age three months ago, and she had just turned fifteen. Just make it happen, Shantaramji, and I will be thoroughly grateful to you for the rest of my life."

Shantaram's heart began to beat hard in his chest. This was the first time in his life he was going against the law of the land. Although he had set up Nirmala's marriage, Tarabai declared that she would only give her daughter to Dheeraj Manoharan, the prospective husband, once the girl finished her twelfth-grade board exams and would officially turn eighteen years old.

"I'll try my best, Khala," whimpered Shantaram, placing Iqbal's photograph in a special blue file that he fished out from his jhola, and replacing it quickly. "Are you sure you don't want to see the proposal I got from Dharavi?"

Khadijah raised herself slowly from the muddy floor, shaking her head from side to side with her eyes closed.

"I certainly don't want anyone but this Iqbal Muhammad Merchant. It's enough that Tarabai's daughter is always in and out of our house, teaching my Amina filthy habits like playing in the garbage, the dilapidated urinal, and what-not. I don't want her to ruin my Amina's married life. Besides, Amina should learn to look after her own affairs."

"As you wish, Khala," replied Shantaram, collecting all the photographs and dumping them quickly into his jhola. "Chalta hu."

Khadijah sighed and entered the inner room to have a drink of water from a mud pot Amina used to fill with water every morning from the local well.

Jaffar, at that point in the day, had finished giving his boss a glass of hot coffee with three teaspoons of sugar in it and had finished dusting the books. He then sat down to bind tattered old books with superglue and tape, wondering what Amina was doing.

Unknown to Jaffar, Amina was sitting inside the dilapidated urinal where the animals of the Bandra Reclamation Slum had made it their mess house and defecation center. She was sitting on her haunches amid the excreta in a gray robe and a black hijab playing her flute to the tune of 'Khuda Khair Kare' from the movie about the famous Delhi Sultan, Razia Sultan, a woman who ruled her people justly ... but was killed because the Royals could not tolerate a woman being their Sultan.

*

Mehndi is a decorative blessing,
In colors red too deep to fade away;
Come and look my friends at my mehndi,
The design is brightening my life anew.
I'm the bride to be wed dressed like a doll,
Mehndi covers the truth of the lines
etched on my palm;
My husband will smell its sweet breath,
And then will he gift his heart at my feet.

Amina's wedding was conducted without pomp or show. Khadijah did not wish to spend any hard-earned money on the third daughter of Jaffar. A pandal was hastily set up with a music deck playing Bollywood songs. The naked street urchins defecated at the entrance of the tent, making Khadijah red with anger.

"Call a shudra and tell him to clean the entrance before the groom arrives. Hurry up! Hurry!"

Luckily for Shantaram, Iqbal Muhammad Merchant wished that Amina should be married to him only after she became eighteen years of age. Therefore, it was after two years that Amina was getting married to her groom from Bhendi Bazaar. Amina managed to attend Nirmala's marriage and helped Tarabai with all the ceremonies, although she was a Muslim and Nirmala was a Vaishnavite Hindu.

Three months after Nirmala's marriage to Dheeraj Manoharan, Amina found herself dressed in bright green bridal finery with her heavily embroidered dupatta covering her full face, while an elderly spinster with black, rotted teeth was decorating her palms and feet with floral mehndi designs.

Mehndi changes your life, my bride,
The colors change during the hues of your life;
Green to red they turn dark to say that you are excited,
While your bridal dress reflects the starry look
in your eyes.

Shantaram, as well as all the Bandra Reclamation Slum dwellers, were running helter-skelter getting things done for the marriage. Jaffar was busy entertaining his guests with glasses of Pepsi and sweetmeats galore. Dr. Rahim Muhammad Sheikh, who could not attend the marriage due to ill health, had sent a giant bouquet of orchids and lilies with a huge Hallmark wedding card congratulating Amina and Iqbal.

The maulvi came in, along with the groom and his family. His two apprentices accompanied him. When some young Muslim girls of the Bandra Reclamation Slum saw

the thirty-four-year-old Iqbal, they all gushed and
beamed.

"He is so tall and handsome. Amina is so lucky."

"Why only praise him? Our Amina is no less a beauty.
See how beautiful her wedding dress is and look at that
mehndi ... so well done and so red."

"They say the redder the mehndi, the more the groom
will love the bride."

"True that! Ha, ha, ha!"

They will tease me about my mehndi,
But only in my heart will I shed my tears;
I'm leaving my mother's house with
a trail of unhappiness,
Quietly like a thief in the night when
the moon does not shine.
My groom may come by horse, elephant, or carriage,
But these tears of shame will I shed from my eyes;
I will preserve this redness till the day I'm home again,
New life brings a sorrow of separation
to the tune of my flute.

Nirmala could not attend Amina's wedding due to a fe-
ver. As Amina sat silently in her bridal dress teased by her
girlfriends of the slum and her cousins, she gulped down
the tears that smudged the cheap kohl makeup applied to
her face. How she longed to play her flute. Khadijah had
packed all her musical instruments in a tin box, which was

placed in her suitcase that she would take to her in-laws. After her tenth-grade board exams, Amina was forbidden to continue her education or go to college. Her father started making her wear her mother's black burka with gloves and socks and a mesh where the eyes could see. Wherever she went, she had to wear that burka, even when filling water from the local well or going to the tiny dairy farm to play her musical instruments.

If only Selma or Mother were alive. How different Amina's situation would have been. The last time she'd seen Dr. Rahim Muhammad Sheikh, on his sickbed on Mohammad Ali Road, he'd mourned with her.

The ceremony ended quickly, *unusually quickly*, thought Tarabai later on when she was discussing the wedding with another Hindu friend. The groom was in a hurry, and so there was no dancing after the main ceremony. When the maulvi asked through a translucent curtain whether Amina was willing to be married to Iqbal Muhammad Merchant, Amina had not answered the maulvi all three times. When the maulvi stared in confusion at Jaffar, he in turn glared at Amina.

Khadijah was the one who saved the situation. "Our Amina is a bit soft, so you didn't hear her say 'qubool hai.' She said it all three times. Amina is our silent one."

Jaffar wiped the sweat from his forehead as the maulvi declared that the wedding was completed legally with the consent of both the bride and the groom. He couldn't

imagine why Amina had not given her consent all three
times and pondered frightfully what would have been the
groom's family's reaction had they realized the truth.

The songs will quell my throbbing heart,
Which bleeds red like my mehndi;
Now here I go away with my husband,
To the land of glass palaces.

The music ended by 1:15 a.m. and a taxi was called to
escort the groom, his bride, and mother to Bhendi Bazaar.
Amina dragged her tiny suitcase, which held her precious
musical instruments, into the taxi and placed it as a di-
vider in the backseat between herself and her husband. By
this time her tears had dried, and it suddenly dawned on
her that she would be on her own from then on, no
abbujaan and no grandmother Khadijah to tend to, and,
for all she knew, her newlywed husband hated music.

Although both Jaffar and Khadijah cried and waved
out to Amina, bidding her goodbye, the bride remained
motionless in the taxi, staring into infinity. The smell of
rotting garbage wafted in the air and entered the taxi,
making the groom twitch his nose.

"What a horrid smell!" he exclaimed rolling up the
taxi's window glass. "This place is the pits. I'm glad I
rushed things, couldn't stand the damn stench in spite of
my expensive attar."

The groom's old mother, extremely thin and flat chested, nodded her head in assent as she pulled up the window glass of her seat next to the taxi driver. "It was a bit too much," she said in a cracked whistling voice, thanks to the fact that most of her teeth were missing. "Good you rushed things up, beta. The food was pretty good, though I've tasted better sweetmeats in my time. The least they could have done was to offer our guests— and us—some kheer or lassi. Their cold drinks too were warm instead of cold, which would have quenched our thirst. It is not a joke to travel in this heat by taxi all the way from Bhendi Bazaar to Bandra Reclamation."

Amina listened to all that was said in her presence. The talk of her husband and mother-in-law unnerved her, but what more could she expect from an uneducated thirty-four-year-old man and his equally illiterate and ill-mannered mother? The mother-in-law, called Munni, turned around to look at Amina as they drove on towards home.

"She is too thin don't you think, Iqbal beta?"

Brashly Iqbal lifted Amina's heavily embroidered dupatta and looked her over. Amina lowered her eyes in shame as she caught sight of the taxi driver staring into the rearview mirror to admire her face with a leering look on his face. After brief scrutiny, Iqbal dropped the dupatta unceremoniously over Amina's head and said, "She is a bit thinner than the photograph that Shantaram showed us, but she is pretty all the same. Fair skin, light brown eyes, and thick pink lips ...”

“But will she do?” implored Munni with a cough.

“Surely, she will do, ammijaan,” replied Iqbal, wiping the sweat from his forehead with his handkerchief. “She has no choice now, does she?”

“True, beta, true,” Munni said with a sigh. She then asked the lecherous taxi driver if he possessed a cigarette or a bidi. The driver steered the taxi with his right hand and, with his left hand, pulled out a packet of Four Square cigarettes and offered it to Munni. She took one cigarette, thanked the driver, and put it to her lips, lighting it with a cheap lighter. Amina began to cough as the cigarette smoke filled the taxi, but she did not raise her head.

Iqbal removed his touch screen cell phone from a pocket in his velvet purple sherwani and began to check his incoming messages. The taxi driver continued to stare at Amina, who was sitting directly behind him, and then he began to scratch his crotch.

*

Tarabai helped Jaffar and Khadijah distribute the rest of the Pepsi and sweetmeats among the Bandra Reclamation Slum dwellers. She also consoled the heartbroken Khadijah, whose tears streamed down her cheeks, not because of Amina’s departure alone, but also because of the way the groom, his mother, and his relations had behaved at the wedding.

"Why were they in such a rush?" she kept on asking Tarabai as Tarabai's sons took down the poles of the temporary pandal. "If they wanted a hush-hush, rush-rush wedding, the least they could have done was to tell us so before we made the preparations. So much food has gone to waste, and I did not like the idea of conducting the mehndi ceremony on the day of the wedding itself. Have you ever heard of such a bizarre thing? It was their wish, so how could we refuse? After all, we were the bride's family."

Shantaram sent his workers to help Tarabai's sons to pull down the pandal. By 2:00 a.m. it was over, but Tarabai and Khadijah sat outside Tarabai's hut, chewing betel leaves along with Shantaram, who was stuffing himself with the leftover pedas. Since he'd been busy helping Khadijah and Jaffar at the wedding, he had not a chance to sit down, relax, and eat the goodies, so he was making the most of it now in the middle of the night.

Khadijah scratched her waist, spat out the red betel juice on the street, and wiped her blood-red mouth with the back of her hand.

"The groom looked a bit too proud, didn't he?" she said.

Tarabai nodded, as did Shantaram.

Khadijah continued her monologue, "But I think he will tame that Amina of ours, and I think she deserves it. Her mother never taught her how to behave like a woman and what a Muslim woman's place in society was. Thank Allah we did not send her to any musical academy, as that idiot doctor who taught Jaffar at school suggested. I managed to train her so much for married life. All praises and thanks be to Allah that this burden is off my back. Now, even if I have to die without seeing my great-grandchildren, I won't mind because I will be going back to my Selma in Jannat."

Tarabai continued to chew her betel leaves in contemplation.

It was Shantaram who broke the silence. "Khala, I'm telling you, this was a good catch for our Amina bacchi, although I would have been happier if they did not have to be in such a rush. They even told the maulvi to speed things up."

"That's the point I was trying to make," said Khadijah, clapping her left palm over her right palm. "I told Tarabai here, as well as Jaffar, when they arrived that something was fishy."

"Not fishy," said Tarabai, ponderously. "*Detached* is a better word. It looked as if he was not part of the sacred ceremony at all. ... Strange very strange."

"Nothing strange, Tarabai," said Shantaram, stuffing another peda into his mouth. "Some grooms are a bit shy on their wedding day but turn out to be great husbands later on. ... Just like Tarabai's son-in-law, Dheeraj Manoharan. Aren't I right, Tarabai?"

Tarabai nodded meditatively, "Dheeraj is another matter. He too is God-fearing and shy, but he treated us with so much respect, and he tried to dance a bit to please us. But Amina's groom ... very strange."

Khadijah pointed her finger at Shantaram.

"Shantaramji, are you sure there is nothing wrong with Iqbal?"

"Hundred percent not, Khala," declared Shantaram. "I swear by the Hindu God Lord Ganesha that there is nothing I have not checked where your son-in-law is concerned. And, Khala, let us not forget, it is you who chose the boy for Amina in spite of me telling you that he earned only 9,000 rupees."

"Yes," mumbled Khadijah, with a slight tinge of regret. "I wanted a handsome son-in-law, but now I wonder whether I have made a mistake. And did you observe the boy's mother? My God, Allah, such a thin woman. As thin as a stick with such yellow teeth. Yuck!"

"I know," added Tarabai. "She looked like a vulture if you don't mind me saying so."

"Oh, not at all," said Khadijah, patting Tarabai's shoulder. "It's not my problem anymore; it's Amina's problem. She had better behave the way I have taught her, or there will be trouble."

"Poor, Amina," moaned Tarabai, shaking her head. "I can't imagine how she is going to live with that woman for the rest of her life. Say, did you also realize something else?"

"What, Tarabai?" asked Khadijah and Shantaram together.

Tarabai whispered her open secret into the night. "The old lady was smelling of tobacco. I know it because I was serving her the Pepsi and sweetmeats."

"Oh, no!" groaned Khadijah, hitting her left palm on her forehead. "My Amina can't stand the smell of smoke. She gets these bouts of coughing whenever she smells even the smoke coming out from a passing vehicle. That's why she used to spend her time playing all her crazy musical instruments on the dilapidated urinal."

"Ugh!" lamented Shantaram, dropping a peda back onto his paper plate as he remembered that the urinal in question had not been cleaned for years. "How could she tolerate the smell of animal excreta?"

"In the same way she had to tolerate life in general," Tarabai said. "Without a mother ... poor soul."

At that thought, they remained silent. After about ten minutes, Tarabai spat out the red betel juice on the road in front of her mud clay hut and entered it to go and catch some sleep. Khadijah, with the help of Shantaram, rose to her feet, and they both dragged their exhausted bodies back to their shanties.

When Khadijah entered her dark shanty, she found her son, Jaffar, sleeping on some rags and crying bitterly. She did not disturb him. She found her way to her side of the shanty, spread out her rags, and lay down to sleep the sleep of the dead.

*

Dr. Rahim Muhammad Sheikh woke with a jolt at 2:15 a.m. He had a fleeting memory of his dream—of white roses stained with so much blood that they died. He wanted to call out to his adopted son, Jumman, but he realized that he could not speak.

His legs and hands felt numb while a headache throbbed in his eyes, ears, and frontal lobe. Again, he tried to call out to Jumman, but he could not find his voice.

At his bedside table sat a glass of water, a tray of biscuits gone soft due to exposure to the atmosphere, and some rare copies of books penned by the nineteenth-century historian Friedrich Max Müller, along with a framed black-and-white photograph of the doctor's father in his graduation robe. The air-conditioner in the room was set low, and the doctor was freezing. He wanted to turn off the cold air and open the windows of his bedroom to let in the night breeze. He tried calling out to Jumman again, but this time he realized that he would never be able to call his adopted son again.

Bookshelves lined the ancient stone walls of the bedroom, containing rare copies of translated Urdu and Arabic treasures, especially books about the Mughal Age, as well as the works of renowned medieval writers like Ibn

Battuta, Abu'l-Fazl, Fa-Hien, Hiuen Tsang, and Babur. The blood in the doctor's veins ran cold, and the darkened room of the meta historian suddenly grew even darker. The doctor could not move, and a sudden ache appeared in his chest. Jumman ... where was Jumman? He had to see him before ...

Books, manuscripts, and periodicals were piled up neatly on the wooden floor. Some periodicals dated back to the nineteenth century, periodicals about Zen Buddhism; the Life of Muhammad the Prophet of Allah; Theosophy; Educational Reforms during the British Rule, and more. All piled one on top of the other, revealing the scholarly mind of the once tall and strong Dr. Rahim Muhammad Sheikh, doctor of medieval history.

Another ache grasped the doctor with its merciless cold hands. His mouth went dry and the room was growing darker. Where was Jumman? Was he pattering down the stairs?

The servants found the doctor in the early hours of the morning, the usual time for him to get up and start his work. They found him with his eyes shut, his mouth half open, and his heart still as a tomb. The once intellectually gifted Dr. Rahim Muhammad Sheikh lay on his bed, dead from organ failure due to old age, his general practitioner would state later.

However, unknown to all except the Almighty, the last word to come from the revered doctor's mouth, the last word he managed to whisper into the darkness descending upon his senses, was the name of the woman he admired and the girl he had failed in this life … "Amina" … "Amina."

CHAPTER TWO

Amina, Iqbal, and Munni's taxi reached Bhendi Bazaar at around 2:30 a.m., the precise time that Dr. Rahim Muhammad Sheikh breathed his last.

Iqbal was busy texting someone on his cell phone, while Munni and Amina were fast asleep, tired from the happenings of the day as well as from the long journey home. The taxi driver parked his vehicle in front of a dilapidated colonial building. It had five floors, and all the residents were Sunni Muslims.

Iqbal checked his cell phone once the taxi drew to a halt. The taxi driver turned his head to address him. "Sir, we have reached your destination."

"At last," groaned Iqbal, placing his cell phone into his sherwani pocket. "I can't wait to relax in the air-conditioned bedroom. The heat is getting worse as the days are going by. Hey, you," he nudged Amina who was fast asleep in her bridal finery. "Wake up, girl, we have reached home."

"Ammi. Oh, ammi," he said, gently shaking the shoulder of his mother, who woke up in a state of fright and smelling of cigarette smoke.

Amina, on the other hand, yawned, rubbed her eyes with both her hands and looked out of the window at her new home, a heritage structure on the verge of collapse. It was a chawl, and its name was engraved in stone along with the date of its erection above the entrance, "Suliman Manzil—1915." The year Mahatma Gandhi returned to India, Amina remembered.

After paying the taxi driver, the handsome and tall Iqbal picked up Amina's old steel trunk and dragged it up the wooden stairs of the chawl. Amina tried to help him, but he raised his hand to stop her.

"No need. I can manage. Just watch your step. The wooden stairs go up in a spiral, and our home is on the top floor."

So Amina let go of the handle of the trunk and followed her husband up the stairs, followed slowly by her mother-in-law. Amina did not fail to notice the taxi driver lecherously staring at her as she timidly, but cautiously, ascended the flight of stairs. She wondered whether she should inform her husband of the driver's behavior, but the thought of her husband's overbearing nature and pride silenced her.

Five minutes later, Amina was in her new home, which had three rooms with a toilet. One room was the kitchen, the other was a sitting room, and the third was a bedroom where the toilet, which stank of urine, was situated.

Munni led Amina into the bedroom. Iqbal had already dumped Amina's trunk on the bed, which had grimy-looking sheets that were old and torn. Munni lifted Amina's dupatta and had a good look at her.

"Hmm ... too young," the old woman muttered, dropping down the dupatta unceremoniously. "Well, take my advice, Amina, listen to and obey your husband at all costs, or believe me, you will be punished for non-cooperation or disobedience. ... Did you get me?"

Amina nodded with a tense look on her face. Punished for what? And what kind of punishment exactly? The old woman stretched her hands and patted her flat, wrinkled stomach.

"Well, it's time for me to rest. I'll see you in the morning then. Amina, dear, don't forget to obey your husband, or else."

After Munni left, Amina shut the door to the bedroom and took in her surroundings. There were no windows in the bedroom, and the walls were heavily padded, giving the room a soundproof appearance. Amina wondered whether the toilet at least had a window, but she dared not interrupt her husband.

No cupboards or study tables, no chairs or stools, and no photographs on the walls . . . just a Samsung box air-conditioner attached to the wall, which had been switched on the moment Iqbal entered the bedroom. To pass the time, Amina moved towards her trunk, opened it, and pulled out the tin box Shantaram had made, where her flute, pipe, and mouth organ were neatly stored.

"A wedding present for my Amina bacchi," Shantaram had stated a few days before the wedding, as he handed the box over to Amina. "May Lord Ganesha bless you and may Lord Krishna, our own bansuri player, help you cultivate your musical talent at your husband's place."

Amina flipped open the box to check whether the musical instruments were safe. They were. As Amina was staring into her precious box, Iqbal flushed the toilet and strode into the bedroom. Seeing the box in Amina's hands, he raised his eyebrows, which wrinkled his forehead. He sneaked up behind her and picked up the box right under her nose.

As he observed the contents of the box, Iqbal said nothing. Amina was hoping he would ask her to play a musical piece for him on her flute or pipe, but her husband closed the lid of the box and handed it back to her.

"So, you are a musician, eh?" said Iqbal. His baritone voice had seduced many a woman. Amina nodded shyly in assent. Iqbal continued, "I see, but Shantaram did not tell me that when he came to us with your proposal." He motioned Amina to place the box back into the old steel trunk, which she did immediately to please him and to avoid the need of any "punishment" that Munni had mentioned.

Iqbal then folded his strong arms and addressed Amina in a voice that sounded like a doctor talking to his patient or a merchant talking to the peon who displayed his goods.

"All right, let's get down to business. Please remove that gaudy dupatta, put it in your trunk, and then stand straight. I want to have a good look at you. Come on, come on, hurry up!"

Amina hastily unpinned the dupatta from her head, folded it, and neatly placed it into her trunk. She then stood straight, staring at her Greek god-like husband, admiring his gray eyes, his dimpled chin, and his muscular arms. Amina hoped he was having a good look at her mehndi, especially the mehndi on her feet.

Iqbal shook his head from side to side very slowly as if he were observing the price of one of the garments on a mannequin.

"Too skinny," he said at last. Then he declared softly, "And your breasts are sagging. Are you wearing a sports bra?"

The bewildered Amina shook her head; she was wearing a regular brassiere.

Iqbal scowled. "Then this is how your breasts generally look. Very well, will do. Now come on," he said pointing his left index finger at her ghaghra choli, "take off all your clothes, I want to see how you look. ... Oh, come on. Don't be shy, speed it up!"

Selma had been the first one in the house at Bandra Reclamation to talk about sex with her younger sisters Maria and Amina. Her limited knowledge was, however, based on the Mills & Boon books she borrowed from her school library. Amina, therefore, knew what was expected of her as a wife where a physical relationship was concerned—yet she felt a bit odd being scrutinized as if she were a commodity.

Nevertheless, she obeyed her stern husband and began to undress. The blouse came off first, then the long ghaghra. Amina folded both and placed them into her trunk.

"Take the bra and underwear off too, please," ordered Iqbal, but this time Amina only stared at her husband queerly. Nothing of what Selma had told her was happening: No soft words of love, no passionate kisses, no embraces, and the man himself did not remove any of his clothes. She felt self-conscious and cold as the air in the room became nippy. She felt like a piece of meat, like something to be sold by Salman Khureshi the local butcher.

"Come on, girl," commanded the impatient Iqbal. "Don't dawdle and squirm like a schoolgirl, just take them off."

Amina bit her lip to hold back the sob in her throat. She slowly took off her bra and underwear, but this time she just let them fall to the wooden floor, which needed to be swept.

Iqbal, with his arms folded over his chest, began to circle his wife. Amina stared at him, incredulous, as he eyed her like a vulture. How she wished he would stop acting weird and start making love to her!

After about three rounds, Iqbal again stood in front of Amina. "Not bad, not bad at all except for the sagging breasts," he said summing up his observation. "All right now, that will do. Go put something else on, and place your trunk under the bed while you're at it."

And with those words, Iqbal Muhammad Merchant left the room. Ashamed and shaken, but thankful that he had gone, Amina dressed in a white salwar kameez with long sleeves to keep her warm. She did not know how to shut off or decrease the temperature of the air-conditioner.

She washed her face in the bathroom. As she expected, there wasn't a window in the toilet, and neither was there a mirror. Amina began to wonder what mess her family had got her into—her husband was so weird and acting strangely. He did not seem to have any affection for her, and what was marriage without love?

Amina thought back to the time when she and Selma discussed what kind of husbands they wanted to marry when they grew up. Selma had adamantly declared that she would marry a man who had some intellect and who was at least a graduate, while Amina just wanted a husband who would allow her to play her music in his house. She pondered whether she should ask her husband when he returned to the bedroom whether she was allowed to play her musical instruments, but the moment he did, she did not have the guts to open her mouth.

When Iqbal, who was now dressed in a sleeveless black singlet and a pair of faded blue jeans, saw Amina standing clueless near the bed, he squinted his eyes at her.

"What are you standing there for, girl? Come on, get on the bed and sleep. You've got a busy day tomorrow, and so do I."

*

"When do you get your periods?" asked Iqbal as he shook Amina awake at 8:15 a.m. The dazed Amina stared at him groggily, feeling rather stupid. Iqbal repeated his question, and the tired girl raised her right hand showing all her five fingers

"On the fifth of every month, eh?" chuckled Iqbal, as he hopped out of bed. "No problem, just asked for the heck of it."

He adjusted his black singlet, while Amina fell off to sleep again. When she awoke, she did not know what time it was since there was no clock in the room, and neither did she possess a watch. The windowless, heavily padded room seemed to eat her up.

Rubbing and flicking the sand from her eyes. Amina jumped off the bed. She visited the toilet and after a wash, dried her face with her white dupatta. She then tried to open the door of the room. To her shock, it was locked. Someone had locked her in from outside.

Amina banged on the door, but no one opened it. She called out to her husband, but there was no answer. How could there be? She recalled as an afterthought that the door also was heavily padded. The room was soundproof. But why?

Amina felt like a white mouse trapped in a cage. Her stomach growled with hunger. Again, she banged the door, but no answer came.

Frustrated and stupefied, Amina decided to do the only thing she could do at that point to calm herself down. She pulled out her trunk from under the bed, grabbed hold of the box, and opened it. She deliberated for a moment, before smiling as she picked up her pipe, shut the box, and placed it back in the trunk. Then she pushed the trunk under the bed.

She sat on the dusty floor cross-legged and began to play the song called "The Sound of Music."

*

With a basket of jute in her hand, Khadijah wobbled to the slum's chicken shop. The shopkeeper gave her a few pieces of meat with a smile. Khadijah haggled over the price, but did not win the argument.

When she returned home, she started to make some Mughlai chicken curry for Jaffar's lunch and dinner.

It had been three weeks since Amina's marriage, but Khadijah still, at times, felt that she could hear the girl playing her flute, mouth organ, or pipe just around the corner. The old lady did not exactly have an 'ear' for music, but she had a rough idea as the years passed by which instrument the third girl of Jaffar used to play most often. She knew that though the girl played three instruments, she loved her wooden flute more than the other instruments.

There had been no calls or messages from Amina in the past three weeks.

"I'm worried, ammijaan," Jaffar had said at the end of the first week. "I hope nothing has gone wrong."

Khadijah had made light of the poor father's anxiousness. "Relax, beta, I bet the girl is too busy doing the groceries, the cooking, the washing, and the other chores of the house to even have time to call us—and if that mother-in-law Munni is what I think she is, she must be busy disciplining our Amina, grooming her into the perfect Muslim housewife. You don't worry your head, she will call us in a few days' time."

However, the call hadn't come. Jaffar tried calling the residents of Suliman Manzil on the landline as well as on Iqbal's cell phone, but his calls had been ignored.

"I'm going there myself to see what's up," Jaffar had declared that day gruffly. "I'll get Shantaram to close shop, get leave from my job for a day, and will go and see Amina."

"Well, don't go empty-handed then," added Khadijah even more gruffly. "Buy some sweetmeats and some tandoori chicken, pack it in a plastic box and—"

"I don't have time for all that!" exclaimed Jaffar. "My-my, it just doesn't seem . . . feel right. I'm going and that's it."

As Khadijah cooked the chicken curry, she prayed that Jaffar and Shantaram came with pleasant tidings about Amina.

*

"Are you sure it's Suliman Manzil and not Suleman Mansion?" asked the electrician and matchmaker Shantaram, tapping Jaffar's shoulder. Jaffar was sitting in front of him, next to the taxi driver who read each building's name on the road in Bhendi Bazaar. He was new to the area.

Jaffar answered Shantaram with a bit of worry in his tone. "I'm the girl's father so I certainly know where they said they stayed, though I've personally not been there myself." He turned to face Shantaram with a skeptical look in his eyes.

"Aren't you supposed to be the matchmaker? You should know the address better than I do."

Shantaram released his hand, which was gripping Jaffar's shoulder. He stammered something about corresponding with the family via e-mail and through another intermediary. This was information that sent a shiver down Jaffar's spine. Jaffar turned around and nervously rubbed his stubble.

The taxi driver was getting annoyed. "Where the heck is this Suliman Manzil? I've been staring out of my window in this heat for the past half an hour," he grumbled. "Are you sure it's a building in Bhendi Bazaar and not on Mohammad Ali Road?"

"Just drive," Jaffar answered, wiping the sweat from his forehead with the back of his left hand.

"You look left, Shantaram, while I look right."

"It will be better if I looked right, Jaffarbhai," replied Shantaram, moving himself to sit right behind the taxi driver, "You look left while I'll look right and, driver sahib, you just keep your eye on the road and make sure you don't knock down anybody."

"Whatever!" groaned the driver, after which he spat out the window.

The taxi driver took a left turn and began to circle the filthy area of Bhendi Bazaar, a Muslim area. Hawkers in dirty kurtas and skullcaps had piled their merchandise on the sidewalks, selling them to the locals of the area. Burkas, hijabs, nightgowns, Islamic flags, sandals, salwar kameez materials, cigarettes, sunglasses, vegetables, fruits, sim cards, secondhand mobiles, school bags, all you could think of were being sold to eager customers, mostly women in black burkas who crowded the streets. The crowd made it very difficult to drive, not to mention claustrophobic.

Shantaram, a vegetarian, gagged as the smells of mutton gosh and barbequed kebabs entered his sensitive nose. He even saw a young Muslim boy selling kebabs attached to sticks on a barbeque stove. Below that, in an open gutter, a stray dirty mongrel was urinating.

"Shantaramji!" bellowed Jaffar. "Look at the buildings, not at the merchandise. I want to see my only child safe and sound."

Shantaram swallowed his spittle with his eyes closed. When he opened them again, he made sure he stared at the derelict buildings and not at the shops and hawkers on the road. He called out the names of the colonial brick and wooden buildings as they passed by.

"Fardeen Manzil 1917, Muhammad Mansion 1930, Akram Hall 1920, Bismillah Rehman Manzil 1942, Naya Daur 1917, Purana Makan 1918 . . ."

"Will you stop that!" yelled Jaffar, staring desperately out of his window. "I'm trying to think."

"By the tiger skin robe of Lord Shiva!" exclaimed Shantaram, "these buildings are so old."

"British built them, sahib," answered the taxi driver. "Whatever they have built have always lasted. See our town area near Fort, what lovely buildings are there, especially the Chhatrapati Shivaji Terminus Station, a beautiful spectacle of great architecture. I'll take you there, sahib? Beautiful buildings ... just beautiful."

"We've not come here for a tour of Mumbai, you fool," growled Jaffar, getting impatient with both of his companions. "Find me that building, Suliman Manzil ... ya Allah, where the heck is it?"

Suddenly, Shantaram screamed in triumph, pointing out of his window.

"THERE IT IS! See... It's engraved in stone: Suliman Manzil—1915. Taxi driver, stop here, please. My... my, what a structure. And it has five floors."

"Yes," replied Jaffar with a contented sigh at last. "Amina's house is on the top floor. Shantaramji, let's make haste."

*

After an exhausting, nerve-racking drive, Jaffar and Shantaram gingerly trotted up the stairs of Suliman Manzil to the fifth floor. They paid the driver and let him go. They decided that when they would be returning home to Bandra, they would take the bus or walk to the railway station – the taxi fare was too expensive.

Shantaram was wearing a light brown khadi kurta over a starched white dhoti. He carried his jhola as well as an unusually large black umbrella, which he stated belonged to his grandfather, making him look like an accountant. Jaffar, though intrigued by Shantaram's 1950s get-up, did not comment. He was preoccupied with thoughts of his daughter's safety. If only he had gifted her a cell phone to communicate with him at every instance! But Khadijah had interfered in that respect as well, saying, "She will not concentrate on her husband and chores if you give her a cell phone, and why spend so much money on her? If she has to call us, she'll use her husband's cell phone or the landline. They do have a landline, don't they?"

Jaffar was not sure now whether they had a landline.

The two men were panting by the time they reached the fifth floor and stood in front of Iqbal's front door. Shantaram rapped the wooden door with his umbrella. It was Munni who opened the door. Upon seeing Jaffar, her jaw dropped, exposing dirty yellow teeth. She reeked of cigarette smoke. Jaffar greeted his in-law with an Islamic salute.

"As-salāmu alaykum Munni ammi, is... is... can I see Amina?"

"Yes, Munni," said Shantaram, joining his hands to form a namaste. "We have not heard from Amina bacchi for three weeks now. I ... I told Jaffarbhai here not to worry, but he insisted—she is after all his only one after ... the tragedy."

With a look of terror still on her wrinkled face, Munni looked from one man to another. Stammering, she called out to her son, not for a moment taking her eyes off the two men in front of her.

"Iqbal munna, your father-in-law and Shantaramji are here to see you. They have come to inquire about Amina."

Jaffar sensed panic in Munni's tone, but for the sake of his sanity decided to ignore it. After hearing a bit of scuffing in the house, Iqbal showed himself. He stood at the threshold of the door right behind his mother. Shantaram tried to get a look into the house but was unable to do so; the room was dark. Iqbal faked a smile at Jaffar.

"Why, Abbujaan, what a pleasant surprise."

"As-salāmu alaykum Iqbal my son," answered Jaffar, a bit confused. "Aren't you supposed to be at work right now, selling your merchandise on the streets? I thought I would see you on my way here. It was a tiresome process to find this building."

"It sure was," added Shantaram, still trying to see deeper into the house. "We went around seven times before I spotted it. Er ... dear ... I mean to say, our dear Jaffarbhai's heart is filled with worry because we have not heard from our Amina bacchi for the past three weeks. As I was telling your mother here, she is his only one, er, where is Amina bacchi, by the way?"

"She isn't at home," answered Iqbal with an indulgent smile that comforted Jaffar's anxious heart. "She has gone to the bazaar to buy herself a musallah and a new niqab after which she will buy some cucumbers for our meal. I must apologize for not getting in touch with you, Abbu, but we've got a hectic life here in Bhendi Bazaar, right, ammijaan?"

"Yes, yes," nodded Munni, the terror suddenly disappearing from her face. "But, but with Amina here, we can manage better, right munna?"

"Absolutely," replied Iqbal with a casual smile. "Amina is the jewel of my eye."

"I'm sure... I'm sure," smiled Jaffar. "She is a special girl, my Amina. Er ... when will she return?"

At this, both Munni and Iqbal were stumped. Shantaram did not fail to notice the hesitation in Iqbal's voice when after a while he answered. "It will take time ... about an hour or so. Don't, don't worry yourself, Abbu, Amina is fine, just busy doing her chores." He put a hand on his mother's brittle shoulder. "My ammijaan is a real taskmaster and is grooming Amina to be the perfect housewife. Aren't you, ammijaan?"

"Yes ... er, yes, of course!" exclaimed Munni, lowering her eyes to the ground. "I try my best."

Shantaram and Jaffar stared at each other. With his gaze, Jaffar tried to tell Shantaram that something was fishy, while Shantaram nodded his head in affirmation as if to say, "You are right. I, too, smell a rat."

Jaffar cleared his throat and said, "May we come in, Iqbal beta and wait for Amina till she comes?"

"I'm ... I'm afraid not, Abbu," stuttered Iqbal, losing his sense of calm. However, he regained it in a flash. "I've not gone to sell my wares today because we are doing the dusting, and since ammijaan is old-fashioned, she does not know how to use a vacuum cleaner. So, I had to stay back. Got to get the place clean for Eid."

Now, it is generally a custom in India that a girl or bride's parents cannot even have a drop of water from their son-in-law's home.

However, Jaffar realized that something was wrong. He, therefore, stared Iqbal in the eye and said, "May we at least have two glasses of water or some refreshing cola? The drive was tiring and the heat was terrible."

Iqbal saw through Jaffar's statement. He smirked and said, "Wait a moment, abbujaan, I'll get you both some cold Coca-Cola from the fridge in the kitchen, or would you prefer Lemonade?"

"Coca-Cola will be fine," murmured Jaffar. "Er... can we wait till Amina returns. It will be a shame to have traveled all this way and not have time to meet my daughter."

"As I said, abbujaan," answered Iqbal calmly, "she will take time to come back home. Maybe an hour or two."

"I can wait."

"Well you can't come inside, you know, it's a mess."

"I'll wait outside on the steps, sipping my Coca-Cola."

"You will be inconveniencing Shantaramji. He may want to get back to his shop."

"He has closed shop to be at leisure to see Amina."

Iqbal grinned from ear to ear. He knew he was stumped.

"Wait here then, abbujaan, while I get the drinks in two glasses for both of you."

"Very well," replied Jaffar in a stern voice that made Munni flare her nostrils in fear. Iqbal left his mother at the door and went inside. After a few minutes, he returned to the threshold with two glasses of Coca-Cola in his hands.

"Thank you, Iqbal," said Jaffar, taking a glass along with Shantaram who was indeed thirsty and so guzzled down the drink very quickly. Jaffar sipped his slowly, looking straight into Iqbal's gray eyes. Iqbal's grin did not fade. Suddenly a mobile phone rang out. Jaffar looked at Shantaram who shook his head as if to say, "That's not my phone." They both then looked at Iqbal, who produced a Blackberry from the back pocket of his blue jeans and held it out to Jaffar. Jaffar saw the phone blinking the name of "Amina."

"But Amina doesn't own a mobile phone!" exclaimed Jaffar with disdain.

"I gifted one to her," replied Iqbal casually. "Go ahead, answer the call, and speak to your daughter."

Jaffar took the mobile from Iqbal's hand and received the call.

"Hello!" Jaffar said, softly. Shantaram put his ear closer to Jaffar and the cell phone so that he, too, could listen to the conversation. Jaffar's eyes glistened with relief.

"It's my Amina!" he said to Shantaram with elation.

"Of course, it's her," said Iqbal teasingly. "Whom did you expect, the Queen of England? Go on ask her all that you want to."

"Hello Amina," said Jaffar, "It is me, abbujaan. Why didn't you call me for the past three weeks? I was worried. Even if you were busy, you should have at least made one call. When will you be back? I'm at your house with Shantaramji... Three hours, but ... but ... Okay, we will definitely come for Eid. Your grandmother is all right. Yes, she cooks well, but not as well as you, my dear. ... I'm so glad to hear your voice. ... Please call me often. The shanty is lonely without you. Hey, Amina, do you play your music here too? Yes, good ... good, I'm glad. ... No, I will go home now, or I'll be inconveniencing Shantaramji. ... Definitely I will come for Eid. ... Yes, my daughter ... yes ... yes. I can hear the commotion in the background. You continue with your shopping. ... Hello ... Hello? Amina, I said you can continue with your shopping. Do not rush, for we will be leaving now ... Yes ... yes ... okay, bye, Amina. Take care and do your chores properly with dedication."

The phone on the other side clicked off, and Jaffar meekly handed the expensive Blackberry back to a very composed Iqbal who put it back in his jeans pocket.

Jaffar finished his Coco-Cola and handed the glass back to Iqbal, while Shantaram gave his to Munni, who was simpering with glee. The two men from Bandra Reclamation apologized and took their leave. Iqbal asked

Jaffar whether he could get an air-conditioned 'cool cab' for them to return home to their slum in Bandra Reclamation, but Jaffar gently refused, saying that he and Shantaram would walk to the station and take a train back home, after which they would hail a rickshaw.

As Jaffar and Shantaram made their way to the railway station, Shantaram said, "You were uselessly worrying. Now you must detach yourself from Amina bacchi. She belongs to her in-laws now and not to you or Khala."

"I'll take your advice Shantaramji," Jaffar said as he maneuvered his way through the crowded street. "You are right. She is no longer my concern. Let her be happy with her husband, and I'll be happy knowing that she is happy."

"Good. You have come at last to your senses," said Shantaram. "Remember, a girl never belongs to the family she is born in, but to the lucky family she is married into."

*

"Have they gone yet?" Munni said, snarling as she took a long draft of her cheap bidi and puffed out the intoxicating smoke into the air.

Iqbal peeked through a crack in the hall window as Jaffar, followed by Shantaram, whizzed through the crowded street of Bhendi Bazaar, away from Suliman Manzil. After about ten minutes, Iqbal shut the window, looked at his mother Munni, and both of them heaved a sigh of relief.

The strapping Iqbal went into the kitchen and grabbed a can of beer from the mini bar. He opened the can and took a long gulp.

"Man, that was a tough cookie—totally unexpected."

"What did you say, munna raja?" asked Munni from the hall.

Iqbal took a sip from the can as he entered the hall.

"I said that their visit was totally unexpected."

"Totally," agreed Munni puffing smoke into the air with relief. "Hey, munna, don't drink all by yourself, go and get me a beer from the mini bar too."

Iqbal smirked, turned towards the kitchen and called out, "Natasha, will you please get another can of beer for ammi from the mini bar?"

After a few minutes, a young woman with an attractive figure and an even more attractive face entered the hall with a can of beer. With a smile, she handed the can to Munni, who opened it with her long claw-like nails. Natasha, wearing a pair of skimpy denim shorts and a lemon-colored tank top that exposed her midriff, went up to Iqbal and kissed him passionately. Munni gulped down some of the frothy drink.

Natasha continued to kiss Iqbal. Her fingers tickled his back while he slid his empty hand into the back opening of her shorts.

Munni brought them back down to earth with an admonishment. "Stop clowning around, you two," she said, "and tell me how you all managed to fool those two idiots from the Bandra Reclamation Slum?"

"Very simple, ammijaan," replied Iqbal, removing his hand out of Natasha's shorts. "When I went to get the cold drinks, I whispered to Natasha, who was hiding there for fear they should see her so scantily dressed, that she should change her name on my phone to Amina. Then while I would be serving those crackpots their cold drinks, she should give me a call from the kitchen, which would register as "Amina" on my Blackberry. She was supposed to lean as close to the open windows of the kitchen as possible and chat with Jaffar as if she were Amina in the marketplace.

"Aha, I see." Munni grinned and took another sip of the drink. "So, the kitchen window's noise of the bazaar downstairs was the noise that those baboons' thought was shouting from Bhendi Bazaar, where Amina was supposed to be shopping? What a hoot! But ... but the voice, Natasha, dear, how did you manage to fool Jaffarbhai with your voice?"

Natasha pulled herself closer to Iqbal, her boyfriend of over three years. "I just imitated her voice from the pleading and screaming sounds I hear from the bedroom when I'm in it. Besides, the girl hardly talks. I don't think she has ever been the chatty one in the family so her father could not make out the difference between my voice and her voice."

"You're right there," said Munni, picking up her bidi. "Shantaramji told me before their marriage that she was well-known as Amina: The Silent One of the Bandra Reclamation Slum. They used to hear more of her flute playing than her voice."

Munni smoked her bidi, which made Natasha's delicate nose twitch. "Not heard her voice here either for the past three weeks, except for some wails, sobs, and cries to let her out of the bedroom. She is certainly a girl without a voice, a mere child, but worth it all the same."

"Except for those sagging breasts of hers," exclaimed Iqbal with irritation in his voice. "All the customers are complaining about that, including Jagmohan the flour grinder, and he is one of our best customers and has always liked the stuff we brought in. We should be more careful next time, ammijaan. Much more careful!"

Munni was about to add her own opinion to Iqbal's cautionary statement when there was a banging on the bedroom door.

"He must be done, baby," said Natasha drawing herself away from Iqbal and going back into the kitchen to hide herself. Iqbal placed his can of beer on a chair nearby and opened the door. Out came the taxi driver who had dropped Munni, Iqbal, and Amina to Bhendi Bazaar on their wedding day. He was panting and sweaty, but smiling a wicked smile as he closed the door behind him. Iqbal helped the taxi driver to a wooden chair to rest himself.

After the man calmed down a bit, Iqbal spoke in a business-like tone of voice. "Well, how was it?"

"Just as I wanted it to be," said the taxi driver, looking up at the tall, handsome Iqbal. "Wish all the husbands of Mumbai were like you. Wow! She was delicious!"

"My payment?" questioned Iqbal, holding out his hand. The taxi driver licked his lips, nodded, and put his hands into his pant pocket, fishing out 500 rupees note. He placed it gently into Iqbal's open palm. Iqbal lifted the note to the light bulb to check its genuineness.

"Hey, bhai," said the taxi driver. "I'm no cheat where it comes to this kind of business. That's a genuine note you got there in your hand or I'm Abraham Lincoln!"

In spite of the assurance given by the taxi driver, Iqbal carefully checked the note in the light after which he placed it in his pocket. "Thank you, and now you may leave," he said.

"Can I come again on Saturday with a buddy of mine?" asked the taxi driver in an excited tone of voice. "He, too, drives a taxi down at Vashi, and he won't mind even parting with 600 rupees for booty like this, your beloved wife."

"You two together, 750 rupees. You or your friend alone, 500 rupees. That is my rate," said Iqbal, sipping his beer. The taxi driver nodded gaily, saying that he would return with his friend on the coming Saturday after work. Iqbal opened the door for him and he left.

"Is he gone, baby?" whispered Natasha from the kitchen.

"Gone, baby doll, in a cloud of ecstasy," said Iqbal. Natasha flew into the room and gave Iqbal another passionate kiss. After a minute, Iqbal took out the 500 rupees from his pocket and handed it to Natasha, who squealed like a girl.

"Go, sweetheart," he said. "Spend it and have fun."

Natasha placed the note inside her bra cup, put on the orange hijab that was lying on the sofa beside Munni, and left the house.

Iqbal finished his can of beer and dropped the can into the dustbin in the kitchen. "Forget your beer," Munni said. "In Jannat's name, go and check on your wife, Amina. See whether she is all right. That blasted taxi driver had his lustful eyes on her the moment we entered the cab on your wedding day. He must have taken the life out of her. Give her something good to eat and be easy on her. She needs you now."

Iqbal nodded at his mother, unlocked the soundproof door of the bedroom, and entered.

*

Mumbai, the commercial capital of India, is a place where some of the most disgusting social evils have risen with their serpent-like hoods to unleash their terrors into the minds of its residents. This city has become a place of high-rise buildings and guilty secrets; business deals and broken dreams; culture and moral degradation. However, what was all that to the eighteen-year-old Amina who lay trapped like a songbird in a cage, naked and humiliated in her husband's bedroom, which reeked with the stench of blood, urine, and excreta? She could not hear the sounds of a bustling city and knew only silence — the silence of the soundproof and windowless bedroom, where she knew neither day or night, time or hour, season or month. Though it came as a shock at first, it had dawned on her that she was a sex slave now. A sex slave sold to different men who would violate her — rape her — humiliate her — kill her slowly every day — from hour to hour, day to day, week to week, month to month.

"Slavery has not ended in India," Amina once heard Selma say. "In fact, according to my social studies book, it has taken the form of sexual slavery where women are used as things, mere things, for the pleasure of vicious males. This book also states that children are not spared the poisonous fang of human trafficking and sexual slavery."

"Will you just shut up?" Khadijah had yelled at Selma. "You must not talk about such things in front of your elders or younger sisters."

"I'm just educating them," Selma had said sarcastically, kneading the dough to make chapattis. "The book also explains how women are bought—actually bought like pieces of meat—by men to be used as sexual slaves."

"Tauba — tauba, won't you shut your blabbering, Selma, and concentrate on your chores?"

Selma had winked at Amina and said softly, "Take care of yourself, Amina, and never, *never* let anyone use you."

"What's that you're whispering to Amina?" Khadijah had said in an irritated tone of voice.

"Just cautioning her, grandmother," replied Selma again, winking at Amina. "Does something weird happen to all Indians when they hear the taboo word *sex*? This is why this is our state today in India, a country where a varied number of goddesses are worshiped, while ordinary women are raped."

"I second the motion," Maria had said, raising her hand, but not taking her eyes off her Paulo Coelho book.

Khadijah had growled. "I'll cut your legs and marry you off, you hear me? By eighteen, both you elder ones will be out of my house and in your in-laws' place!"

Selma rolled her eyes and continued to knead the dough, making Amina laugh.

Selma — appa (elder sister) Selma — gone before she could even finish her matriculation, and now — Amina — nude and tied to the bed's poles with ropes that cut her tender fair wrists with blood trickling down her hands.

Yes, Amina was now a sexual slave who had been continuously raped and violated by a number of men who could pay her "husband." The first time it happened, Amina screamed and bled so badly that Natasha had to be called in to calm her down with sarcastic warped words of comfort.

"Relax, doll face. It only hurts the first time, you know," Natasha had murmured while Amina's husband stripped and tied her to the bed. "No need to worry. Have fun, relax, and help your hubby to earn more money. Isn't it a wife's duty to make her husband happy? Well, take my advice and live it up, doll face."

Her husband never used her at all for sex. Instead, he treated her like a laboratory mouse. He was very civil and yet very cruel at the same time.

After every rape by other men, Iqbal would enter the soundproof bedroom, which muffled all the shrieks and screams Amina made. He would enter the bedroom, switch off the air-conditioner and ask routine passive questions.

"How are you doing, Amina?"

"I'll be sending some food with Natasha in here in about half an hour's time; would you also like to have a soft drink?"

"Do you want me to help you wash, or do I send Natasha in for that?"

"If you would co-operate and not scream all the time, I wouldn't have tied you to the bed, you know, and then you could use the toilet whenever you wanted instead of messing my bedroom up."

"Would you like a sip of brandy?"

"Anything you need?"

Amina would beg him to let her go. She would plead, cry, and howl, to no avail. She was a prize not to be lost, a beautiful prize, and the calculating Iqbal was going to make maximum use of her.

At first, Amina was able to count the number of times her husband's "customers" had violated her, but by the end of the second week of her marriage, Amina stopped counting and even stopped screaming for help.

The day when the taxi driver violated her, her husband entered the soundproof bedroom, gingerly making sure he did not step into any puddle of urine or blood. With her hands tied, Amina lay at the foot of the bed, dark circles under her eyes and her whole fair naked body covered with the taxi driver's teeth marks.

"Ya Allah!" exclaimed Iqbal, hitting the palm of his left hand to his head. "Look at what the blasted fellow has done to my merchandise. His teeth marks are all over your body. Good heavens ... eew!"

When he turned Amina's head to face him, he saw that the beastly taxi driver had chewed the left lobe of Amina's ear to such an extent that the flesh was a mangled bundle of blood and skin.

"That monster! HE HAS RUINED MY PROPERTY! Hang on, Amina! I'll return with a quack from the local bazaar, don't worry. I'll be back!"

When the quack had a look at the earlobe, he shook his head and then looked up at the frantic Iqbal.

"Sorry, boss, the man who did this has damaged it beyond my medical capabilities. The teeth marks will heal, but it will take about three to four weeks. I'll bandage the earlobe, but that is all that can be done. Take my advice and don't let that taxi driver back in here for another century if you want your goods to be shipshape for customers."

The quack then applied some tumeric powder on Amina's ear and bandaged it up.

Iqbal was furious. "I'll sue that creep for doing this to my property. Ya Allah, three to four weeks! Who the hell will feed me some cash in those weeks of want?"

The quack took a closer look at the expressionless zombie that was Amina. He measured her breasts with his hands, ran his hand down her bare back, and licked her lips.

He then turned towards Iqbal and said, "My men and I will pay 340 rupees each for a taste of her till she gets cured, and I guarantee you that they will be gentle on her. Deal?"

"Deal," exclaimed Iqbal, shaking the quack's hands. "Thank you. Thank you so much. Believe me, she is a real Barbie Doll."

"That is why I made the offer," replied the quack, winking at Iqbal. "I'll come by in the evening with 340 rupees for a bit of fun for myself, and if another of my fraternity is available, I'll get him along with his money as well."

"Be my guest," Iqbal said.

Amina let a tear roll down her face.

When the quack left, Iqbal entered the soundproof bedroom and sat on the dirty bed next to the stand to which Amina's wrists had been tied. He coughed, trying to gain her attention, but her lifeless eyes stared at the floor. When he called her name, she lifted her legs, bent them at the knees towards her breasts, and tried to hide her nakedness.

For a brief moment, Iqbal felt a twinge of sadness for his slave-wife, but the feeling disappeared as swiftly as it had come. He went near her, but as he did so, she screamed.

"Okay, okay!" he said, raising his hands in the air. "I won't touch you, Amina. You know that I don't look at you in that manner. You are my wife, my possession, and I'll be the last person to harm you. You, er... you want to eat something?"

Amina tried to free herself from her bonds but only cut her wrists in the bargain, yet again. Iqbal pointed to the bonds,

"You know that I can take them off only if you promise not to scream, shout, hit me, or try to leave the room. Come on, Amina, be a sport. You know I'm way better than most other husbands. I'm polite, I'm kind, I don't yell at you, and I don't use you. So, how about it? Let's take those bonds off, and you be a good wife and all."

Amina raised her downcast eyes and looked into her husband's gray eyes. She at once understood what she saw in those eyes. It was the same emotion a Muslim felt when he was about to cut the neck of a goat for Bakri-Eid. She never did like that festival. And she did not like her husband.

After futile efforts to free herself and in the bargain reddening her flesh, Amina groaned in agony.

Iqbal again asked, "If you promise to behave yourself and not to hit me, I will take off those bonds. Scout's honor!"

Once again, Amina looked into Iqbal's gray eyes, and tears began to drop down her cheeks, breasts, and thighs.

With the resignation of the defeated, she held out her bonds towards Iqbal, who with a grin began to untie the rope. Once they were off, Amina stretched her arms and clicked her fingers, staring at the ground tiles. She saw to her horror that the ground had been stained with her urine, blood, and excreta.

Iqbal followed her gaze. "Yes, it's a mess," he said, shrugging his shoulders. "Do you want to play the good housewife for a while? You can have a wash and change, and then I'll help you clean up the mess but," he said, raising his left index finger, "one false move to escape, and the bonds will go back on."

Amina glared at Iqbal. She covered her chest with both her hands, crossed the room, and entered the toilet to wash. Iqbal waited about fifteen minutes before a cleaner Amina, her light brown hair wet, emerged from the toilet, a towel covering her modesty.

Iqbal, by that time, had dragged Amina's trunk from under the bed and had taken out a long-sleeved ebony salwar kameez, along with a black brassiere and black underwear. He had placed the clothes on the filthy bed along with the small tin box where her musical instruments were kept safe and sound.

Amina, as if in a trance, changed right in front of Iqbal. Once she was dressed, both man and wife started to swab the floor until the room smelled of cleanser.

"Well," said Iqbal, satisfied, "that's more presentable for the customers." Turning to Amina who was sitting cross-legged on the bed, her lips quivering, he asked, "How is your earlobe? Does it hurt really bad? Do you need to see a real doctor?"

Amina absentmindedly touched her left lobe. Her eyes had a glazed look about them. Yes, the earlobe hurt, but her vagina hurt more, not to mention her soul. She did not reply. Iqbal tossed his hands up in the air in frustration.

"Woman, don't you ever talk? You have been in my house for over, let me see, yes, three and a half months, and other than your screams, wails, hollers, you've not said anything much. Were you this quiet at your father's home too?"

Amina merely nodded her head in affirmation, very slowly as if each nod cost her money.

"There we go again," said Iqbal, rolling his eyes. "You don't open your mouth and say yes. You nod your beautiful head like a bull. Is it a family trait to be so silent?"

Amina smiled weakly to herself, thinking of Selma. Oh, if only her husband had met Selma, she would outwit him and maybe punch his nose for his high-and-mighty behavior.

*

"I will wallop my husband if he annoys me," Selma once said, in the middle of solving mathematical equations. "I won't take any of his nonsense. I will be a self-made woman of the twenty-first century."

"I second the motion," Maria had said and got a kick on the back from Khadijah. "Ow, grandmother, that hurt!"

"It better hurt!" Khadijah said as she massaged Afsheen's soft body with baby oil. "And both you elder ones better stop talking nonsense. Remember, there is no such thing as a 'self-made woman.' We have to listen to our elders and our husbands at all times whether we like it or not."

Then turning to Jaffar, Khadijah said, "Ask him. Ask your father. His father, that means your grandfather, used to at times slipper me, sometimes for the flimsiest reasons. He would beat me up, if there was a strand of my hair in the dhal or if his bath water was not made hot enough or if I had neglected to massage his head."

"Eesh," exclaimed Selma with disgust still focused on her mathematics notebook. "Then thank Allah grandfather died before I was born. What an MCP. I wouldn't have tolerated him for a minute!"

Amina, Jaffar, and the wife of Jaffar had giggled, but Khadijah looked confused and innocently asked, "What is this MCP now?"

"Male Chauvinist Pig," Maria had answered, though her eyes remained fixed on her novel by Dean Koontz.

"Kya-kya-kya?" Khadijah had repeated rapidly like a parrot, which made Selma burst out laughing holding her tummy. Rahat had smiled at her husband, and he had kissed her cheek.

Seeing her son showing affection to his wife had sent a chill up Khadijah's spine. "No kissing in front of the children. You have forgotten your manners Jaffar. Remember no kissing, hugging, or touching your wife in front of elders and children."

"That's why our population is overtaking China's," Selma had said sarcastically. "When Indian couples are alone from so-called 'elders' and 'children' to whom they can't show affection, they make the most of it and then produce another child. We may mock the west, but if you ask my opinion, it is India that is more obsessed by 'sex' than any other country."

This made Khadijah fume. "How many times have I told you not to use that filthy word in front of elders and children!"

"What word?" Selma had said with a chuckle.

"What word?" Maria echoed.

"What word?" the wife of Jaffar had repeated, kissing Jaffar's cheek, so that Jaffar looked mischievously at her and said, "What word?"

"Wha wo?" Feroza, the infant, had repeated, gurgling with glee, her spittle splashed all over her pink face. Then everyone had laughed except Khadijah, who growled the forbidden word like an abuse under her breath.

"Sex!" she said, but she pronounced it more like *she-axe.*

*

"You're smiling to yourself," Iqbal said tenderly bringing Amina back to her reality. No Selma... no Maria... just Iqbal, herself and her shame. She began to weep.

"Hey, hey, hey," Iqbal exclaimed. "I thought we promised we weren't going to cry?"

Amina choked down her tears, but the memories of her two elder sisters clouded her fair face with a shadow so dark that for a minute it looked as if Amina would die. And at that moment, with the ache in her vagina and the bite marks on her body, Selma ... Maria ... how she wished to return to them!

Iqbal saw that Amina was going to cry again so he tried to take her out of that mood, but was unsuccessful until he said, "Okay, okay let's talk about art, dance, sculpture, poems, and music."

Amina raised her head with a jerk. She turned her eyes and stared at the tin box where her musical instruments lay.

Iqbal smiled his best smile. "How about you play me something on your musical instrument? I can't play any musical instrument myself, but I am a good singer ... or that's what people say. Here take your box." Iqbal picked up the box and handed it to Amina, who grabbed hold of it and clutched it to her chest, looking into Iqbal's gray eyes with trepidation.

"Go on, open it, and play me something," urged Iqbal gently. "I'm not going to hurt you as long as you co-operate with me ... which you are doing so right now by not screaming, shouting, etc., so go ahead, play."

Amina, thus assured, nodded her head and then flipped open her box. There lay her wooden flute, her mouth organ, and her metal pipe. She picked up her favorite, the flute. Iqbal relaxed on the bed, cradling his head with his left hand while Amina positioned herself cross-legged on the now clean floor.

She began to play. Iqbal was geared up and ready to hear some childish tunes of do-re-me or "Mary Had A Little Lamb," but what he heard made his jaw drop. Amina's long delicate fingers raced across the flute with precision, and to Iqbal's shock, he realized that Amina was playing a complex raga.

The music of the flute brought a feeling of awe and amazement in Iqbal's mind. He had listened to many ragas in his time, but none sounded so mesmerizing as the one he heard his wife playing before him. Her eyes were shut, and her fingers were moving spryly.

The music made Iqbal feel as if he were near a babbling brook somewhere in Kashmir, with snow falling all around him. The raga gave him a sense of enlightenment – of peace and serenity—and for the first time, humility.

For ten straight minutes Amina played, before Iqbal realized that this raga was only a prelude to yet another song, which Amina began to play slowly, softly, with her eyes opened and tears running down her face.

Now the song sounded quite familiar to Iqbal, but he couldn't put his finger on which one it was. Was it an English rock song? Was it a Bollywood song? Was it a Shloka? What was it?

Then, like the hand of death over an ailing body, Iqbal suddenly realized what song his wife was playing. He had heard it many times whenever he went with the Catholic Natasha to church. It was a church hymn, and the lyrics made him self-conscious.

Abide with me; fast falls the eventide;
The darkness deepens; Lord, with me abide;

. . . In life, in death, O Lord, abide with me.

Amina stopped playing, but her tears still trickled down her face. Iqbal sat up straight as if he had been stung by a bee.

They stayed like that in silence for five minutes until the bedazzled Iqbal said, "Play ... play another one, another hymn, with the... the raga. Another one, please."

Amina wiped her tears with her dupatta and dabbed at the snot on her nose. She then played another enchanting raga, her fingers moving fast and effortlessly along the flute.

This time Iqbal felt as if he were in a forest in the rain that drenched the earth, its scents rose to his nose and took him to a land of wild deer and the realm of the Bengal tiger, who searches for a place to rest.

After a long prelude, Amina began playing another Catholic hymn that embarrassed Iqbal to the bone, making him turn his eyes away from his wife in shame.

O Lord My God, Why Have You Gone from Me?
Far from My Prayers, Far from My Cry,
To You I Call, But You Never Answer Me,
You Send No Comforter, and I Don't Know Why.

When Amina stopped playing the second hymn, she began to weep again.

"You ... you play so beautifully!" stammered Iqbal, staring uneasily at Amina, who placed the wooden flute back in the box and covered her face with her hands and wept uncontrollably.

*

"What a crybaby!" Selma had once said when she was bottle-feeding Afsheen, her little sister. "Amina was so much better when she was an infant. Remember, ammijaan?"

Rahat would smile her trademark dimpled smile with Amina playing the scales on her flute sitting on her lap. Rahat would run her fingers through Amina's gorgeous hair with pride and affection.

"Dekhna, my Amina will become a great musician. People from all over the world will crowd to listen to her play her flute. Dr. Rahim Muhammad Sheikh Sahib promised me that he would send my Amina to a music school."

"I know," Selma would reply rolling her eyes. "You have been telling us that for so many years now, but you have not got down to doing it."

"It's not the right time yet," said Rahat, tying a plait with Amina's hair. "She is only six years old. Let her at least turn ten and a half; then you'll see what great heights my third girl will reach with her music."

"Whatever, ammijaan!" Selma would say mechanically, staring at the amount of milk that was being drunk by her infant sister.

Amina remembered everything: the warmth of her mother's lap, the scent of her infant baby sister Afsheen, the sarcastic but indulging tone of Selma, and the hope— all lost, all lost.

*

Iqbal was uneasy. For the first time in his life, he realized what he had done was worse than any sin Allah could cook up. Amina was a musical genius ... a genuine musical genius, and what had he done? He had made her a sexual slave. He had allowed other men to use her. He allowed her to be raped right under his roof, he had . . .

"Munna beta, what are you doing so long inside the soundproof room?"

Iqbal jumped off the bed, as his mother called out to him in her loudest voice. "Munna raja, are you having fun with the goods? You know you are not supposed to use the goods for yourself. She is only for customers. Get out of the room, or I'll choke her to death, so help me I will!"

*

Iqbal paced up and down the hall. Natasha leaned against a wall, bored, her hands folded over her white tank top, and one eyebrow raised.

The door of the soundproof room was locked with Amina inside dressed in her black salwar kameez playing her flute.

Munni, who was grinding her teeth in rage, spit out her words with venom, "What do you mean we have made a mistake? We got her married to you fair and square for our prostitute and trafficking business. She is not the first, and she will not be the last, Munna, so stop having feelings for the goods. She is just a girl!"

"No, ammi." Iqbal stopped his pacing, "She is not like the others I have worked with and then eventually sold." He blinked his eyes several times and began to shiver, although it was the middle of summer. "She ... she is a musician; she plays the flute like an angel from heaven."

"So what!" growled Munni, lighting a cigarette and puffing smoke into the air like a chimney. "I don't care if she even plays the flute like the Hindu God ... er ... what's his name?"

"Krishna, ammi," answered Natasha with a sneer, her eyebrow still raised.

"Right, Lord Krishna," exclaimed Munni triumphantly. "I don't care about her artistic talents. She has got her looks, her pretty face, and a young body, which I intend to make maximum use of until she can be sold to my takers in Rajasthan." Munni raised herself from the sofa, dragged her feet to where Iqbal was standing, and caught hold of his kurta sleeve, shaking him vigorously, "You are not the boss of this business! I am." Her cigarette stuck out of her mouth.

She slapped Iqbal twice on both cheeks, "That Amina is our bread and butter. I've been doing this business since the 1970s when you were nothing but a tiny toddler. I brought you up, single-handedly, though I was not married, so that you would aid me in my business and aid me you shall."

Munni then slapped Iqbal once again so hard that his eyes began to water. Natasha smiled to herself. Iqbal held his reddened cheek and stared at the thin but strong body of his mother.

This was the person who had been beating him up since he was a child. He was never sent to school and was forced to bed a woman at age fourteen, much before his time . . . and the lust had not left him since then. His very own mother introduced him to the prostitution and human trafficking scenario. Amina was not the first so-called wife he "married" to be used as a sex slave. There had been others ... many others. ... Some as old as Amina, some younger and once in a while, little innocent child brides.

Munni taught him not to get emotional, indeed, also not to bed any of the women/girls himself so that they would be fresh for special customers who preferred virgins. Those who liked to tear hymens ... and those who liked a little spilling of blood in their sexual activity.

Yes, Amina was just a girl, but the music of the flute still rang in his ears, making him for the first time feel a twinge of guilt in his immortal soul. He could not let anyone rob her of her dignity anymore. Not Amina.

"No, ammi," whimpered Iqbal with resolution. "I will not allow any man to touch her ever again. She ... she is a musical genius, a maestro."

Munni puffed out smoke from her nose and mouth. Natasha spoke this time, "Okay, honey, then what exactly do you want us to do with Amina? We can't send her back to her father because she will tell what has happened to her, and now you do not wish to even use her for business." She swayed towards Iqbal and caught hold of his muscular arm. "So, baby, we are in the soup, aren't we?" The fingers of her left hand traveled slowly towards Iqbal's crotch. "So what is your plan, baby boy? Are you going to forget ammi and me?"

"No, baby, no!" said Iqbal, taking Natasha into his arms. "I'm only yours. You don't need to worry, and business will go on as usual. All I have to do is get married again to another girl."

Munni puffed out more smoke, and in her characteristic whistling voice she muttered, "And what exactly do you want to do with Amina? Make her into the next Lata Mangeshkar, oh la de la da!"

Natasha chuckled, and Iqbal naughtily put his hand under Natasha's neon pink skirt and rubbed her buttocks. Natasha then casually removed her white tank top and her white sports brassiere. She rubbed her nipples and Iqbal began to kiss her passionately. Munni hit her left palm on her forehead in frustration,

"Ya Allah, what a splendid time they have decided to get intimate when my whole business is at stake, all because my son thinks that that brat in the bedroom is a musical genius."

Munni sat back on the sofa and put on the radio that lay next to her. As she lay down on her back, smoking her cigarette and listening to some modern Bollywood songs, the passionate couple next to her shamelessly removed their clothes and made love on the floor.

Inside the soundproof bedroom, however, Amina sat cross-legged on the floor with the mouth organ to her lips and played an English song she learned in the singing class at school called "*At the Beginning with You.*" As she maneuvered her fingers and mouth over the mouth organ, she remembered Maria, the only singer in the family, singing the song in her soprano voice, sitting next to a tiny Amina with a Mills & Boon book in her hand.

We were strangers starting out on our journey
Never dreaming what we'd have to go through
Now here we are and I'm suddenly standing
At the beginning with you.
No one told me I was going to find you
Unexpected what you did to my heart
When I lost hope, you were there to remind me
This is the start.

*

Munni, at last, gave in to the whims of her son. In a month's time, Iqbal married another girl from Vashi—a sixteen-year-old Muslim teenager called Noor—and caged her up in the soundproof bedroom just like Amina had been caged up with customers arriving daily to make use of the poor helpless child.

Amina was released from the bedroom with strict instructions from Iqbal in his usual business-like voice not to give them away and never to leave the house or scream under any circumstance. Amina, though weary and shattered from within, gladly accepted the ground rules.

In the beginning, Munni was skeptical, and while Iqbal was out of the house selling nightgowns on Mohammad Ali Road as a pretense occupation, the bony old lady taped Amina's mouth shut with construction tape and made her sweep as well as swab the house clean. Iqbal put an end to this practice, knowing that Amina without her mouth free wouldn't be able to play her musical instruments. When he did this, Munni grew angrier and Natasha grew suspicious.

Once her chores were done, Amina comforted Noor in the soundproof bedroom and helped her clean herself whenever she was not with a customer. Otherwise, by 5:00 p.m., Amina would remove one of her musical instruments, sit at Munni's feet, and begin to play.

The first time Munni heard Amina play her flute she was mesmerized.

"The girl's fingers literally fly over the flute, producing such soothing music to the ears," Munni told Iqbal.

"I told you, but you wouldn't listen."

During these talks, Amina said not a word but washed the dishes noisily, remembering Selma, Maria, and her mother often during the stillness of the night. While the rest of the family would fall asleep during the early hours of dawn, Amina would lock herself up in the kitchen and play her pipe. She preferred playing her pipe during that period.

One day, as a customer was paying Munni the usual 500 rupees for Noor, Iqbal burst into the house calling out to Amina.

"Hey, Amina! Amina, I've got some news for you."

Amina looked up from swabbing the floor under the strict supervision of Munni.

"It's your best friend, Amina ... Nirmala," Iqbal continued. "Nirmala is with child. Your father just called me on my cell phone to give me the good news. She is three months pregnant."

Amina's face curved into a smile, but no sooner did she recall her own situation than she began to shed silent tears and resumed swabbing the floor. Iqbal, saddened when Amina did not react, shut the door behind him and returned to his job.

Munni giggled fiendishly at her customer with the 500 rupees note in her hand and said, "Children are pests. Iqbal was a pest too, but because he would be useful for my business I held on to him."

Amina did not say a word and silently prayed in the shrine of her big, forgiving heart that Nirmala would give birth to a boy and not a girl.

*

In the third month of Amina's release, Munni was smoking a cigarette while Amina was asleep at her stinking feet. Suddenly there was a frantic knocking on the front door. Both women jumped up. Munni's cigarette fell from her mouth. She thought the police had come for her. The knocking continued.

"Don't! Don't open the door," stuttered the old lady in a whistling voice. Her nerves calmed down only after she heard Iqbal's voice coming from the other side of the door.

"Hey, ammi ... Amina, open the door. It's just me. I've brought something special for my wife, Amina ... jaldi daarwaza kholo."

Timidly, Amina went towards the door and opened it with a creaking sound that irritated Munni no end. Iqbal entered with a huge rectangular box in his hands. Amina shut the door behind him as he placed the box on the floor. Munni rolled her eyes.

"What did you get her, a hookah?" she said.

"Ammi," said Iqbal indulgently. "Is smoking the only thing you think of?" He was smiling his best smile, which was normally reserved only for Natasha—and Munni did not like it.

Iqbal continued, "Ammi, I want Amina to be able to develop her musical talents. She can become ... I don't know, a concert player? A musician?"

"You first tell me what's in that damn box," Munni said with a grunt.

In answer, Iqbal looked towards Amina and motioned her to open the box. Amina, curious, went down on her knees in her long-sleeved white salwar kameez and slowly opened the lid of the rectangular box. It was a Casio.

"GOOD HEAVENS!" screamed Munni, beating her head with her hands. "Not another musical instrument! It must have cost a bomb."

"No it didn't," replied Iqbal tartly. "I got it cheap because the man who was selling it was one of our best customers, and he is enjoying Noor. Hey, Amina," cried Iqbal, snapping his fingers in front of her face, "go ahead. Explore, play it, and I'll try to get a music teacher to teach you."

"Over my dead body!" howled Munni. "You are crazy, Iqbal! CRAZY! Don't you know how secretive we have to be about our business? If another person enters this house, he or she will grow suspicious and will report us to the police. Then you, Amina, and I can sit together and clap our hands like eunuchs over our misfortune."

"Don't overreact, ammi," whined Iqbal like a schoolboy.

Munni slapped Iqbal and pulled his dark brown hair until it hurt. Iqbal tried to push her back, but she stuck to him like a leech, abusing him in the foulest language possible.

Amina, on the other hand, began to play the keys of the Casio with her right hand. Although she did not know any of the black or white keys by name, she recognized them by the sound they made. By the time Munni had kicked Iqbal in the shin and he howled in pain, Amina was playing the major scale on the piano that is "Do Re Mi" as well as the heptatonic scale of Indian Music "Sa Re Ga Ma Pa."

Due to Munni's objection, a music instructor was not found for Amina, but the girl, who was soon to turn nineteen, had begun to play many songs on the Casio, though only with her right hand.

Amina played her Casio, which was battery operated, every time she was free. She played to an audience consisting of Munni, Iqbal, and sometimes the jealous Natasha. Thanks to the recording button of the Casio, Amina learned, with a little help from Iqbal, how to record her Casio chords beforehand and then play it along with her flute, mouth organ, or pipe. In two weeks' time, Amina learned how to play thirty-two songs—which made Munni marvel at her.

"Maan gaye bhai, Jaffar's daughter seriously turned out to be a prodigy ... a musical prodigy."

However, not all was serene. Iqbal's latest wife Noor, due to having intercourse too often, had begun to bleed terribly from her vagina, and she began to hallucinate. She was getting deranged and anemic, but Munni nor Iqbal dared not call a doctor in. Instead, they called in the same quack who tended to Amina's ear.

The quack did a brief examination of the sixteen-year-old with mangled hair sleeping completely naked and tied with ropes to the bed. The quack shook his head, just as Iqbal had expected him to.

"No, she has got an internal injury in the uterus, which is not good. She won't be able to have intercourse with anyone. If she does, she dies."

"Ya Allah!" moaned Munni, staring at the unconscious Noor on the bed in the soundproof bedroom. Iqbal and Natasha were there too. Natasha felt nauseated when she smelled the warm blood that had drenched the dirty bedsheets where Noor slept soundly. Natasha, clad in only in a pair of khaki shorts and a black brassiere, stared at the girl on the bed, eight years her junior. She could see gray streaks already appearing in Noor's hair.

Iqbal scratched his head in deep contemplation. *What were they to do now? They couldn't keep her. Surely their business would suffer. They couldn't send her back to her parents' house in Vashi – hah! – They would be locked up immediately. No one would buy a lunatic for sexual enjoyment ... or would they?*

Iqbal tapped the quack's shoulder. The man was taking advantage of Noor's condition, massaging her breasts and kissing her passionately. Iqbal punched him in the stomach, and the quack quickly calmed the erection that Natasha could plainly see in his dhoti.

He apologized, "So sorry, boss, but you know how it is when there is a naked woman in front of you—you just can't control your instincts, now can you?"

Iqbal and Natasha exchanged knowing glances.

Munni, who was beside herself with rage, said, "I DON'T CARE ABOUT YOUR BASE DESIRES, YOU IDIOT! Tell me what I can do with her before she dies or gives our game away! Hurry up. I've got a business to run!"

The quack looked over once more at Noor and pondered for a while, after which, he said, "I'll take her to one of our ashrams where they treat ... or pretend to treat, the mentally ill. The fee will cost you, but if she is admitted there ..."

"Where is this ashram?" asked Munni.

"In Old Delhi. Many celebrities donate their spare cash as charity to the ashram ..."

"But it is actually a sex den where the helpless are made use of by the ashram workers," mumbled Munni, nodding her head in recognition. "I remember that it was set up after the death of our first lady prime minister Indira Gandhi." She then slapped her thigh and said, "Very well, we will send Noor there. What's the price and how do we benefit?"

"One moment, madam," said the quack. He fished into his jhola and after much searching, found an old brochure. He handed it to Munni, but she declared she could not read. He then tried to hand it to Iqbal, but he also stated that he could not read.

"Give it to me, you fool," said Natasha, grabbing the brochure. "I'll read it."

After reading the first two sides, Natasha's jaw dropped in shock.

"What is it?" cried Munni. "What is the entry fee?"

Natasha looked at Iqbal and sheepishly answered, "50,000 rupees for a lifetime stay."

"Nahi!" screamed Munni, beating her chest with both hands. "I'll be ruined." In a rage, she kicked the blood-stained bed three times. With a bony finger, she pointed accusingly at Iqbal. "This is your entire damn fault. We were making good money with Amina. BUT YOU DO NOT WANT HER TO BE USED ANYMORE! 50,000 rupees ... 50,000 rupees. That's two months' pay we get from our obliging customers."

She pulled at her hair and shrieked, cursing Iqbal. "BLAST YOU, FIEND, TAKING AN OLD WOMAN'S MONEY FROM HER AFTER SHE HAS DONE

EVERYTHING FOR YOU... 50,000 rupees ... Allah have mercy, 50,000 rupees!"

"Madamji, calm down," said the quack. "Your bahu has not read the whole brochure."

"She is not my bahu!" growled Munni. "Just my son's mistress."

"Hey, I'm his true love, ammi!" answered Natasha with a whine.

Munni ignored her and panted, clutching her heart.

The quack continued in a pacifying tone of voice. "Madamji, calm yourself. I'll tell you ... the brochure also states that if the patient is on her deathbed, the fee is reduced. Then it is only 25,000 rupees."

With a frenzied look on her face, Munni darted her yellow eyes from the quack to Noor on the bed. She then asked, "Is ... is Noor going to die?"

"Well, not really," said the quack with a leer. "But I can make her reach that stage with a few of my special methods, which will in any case not cause alarm where the police are concerned. I assure you that I can damage the vagina and uterus to such an extent that she will have no choice but to die after a brief stay at our peaceful ashram."

Munni, at last, smiled, her gleaming dark yellow ratty teeth making the quack want to retch.

"Excellent, excellent!" she snarled. "Do it. Do whatever you want, but get rid of her so that my business may not stop. Iqbal!" she ordered with her gnarled finger, pointing towards him. "Withdraw 15,000 rupees from the bank and give it as an advance to our dear quack here – the rest of the money will be paid after the job is done. Now go!"

*

Amina was sitting cross-legged in the hall on the floor. She was wearing her black salwar kameez, which stank of perspiration. Her flute was in her hands, but she only petted it and not once put it to her lips to play. Her eyes were moist and red, but she blinked her tears away. Her face was pale, her cheekbones prominent, and she was cold, very cold. She remembered Selma yet again.

"Such people should be stoned to death!" Selma had said as she read *The Times of India* about the infamous rape of a young Delhi student called Nirbhaya. "Or better yet, their genitals should be cut off. Bloody beasts!"

"No using foul language in front of the younger ones!" admonished Khadijah, preparing her paan while Amina, then seven years old, massaged her grandmother's back. "The more she reads and studies, the more that word *bloody* (Khadijah pronounced it as *blue-dee*) comes to her mouth. Get up from the damn floor and help your mother clean the vegetables."

Selma, however, continued to read. After a few minutes, she squealed. "Yuck, yuck, bloody yuck!"

"What did I just tell you?" scolded Khadijah.

"But listen to this, grandmother," replied Selma in a fury. "One of the minor boys who gang-raped Nirbhaya on a moving bus took an iron rod—and pushed it into her vagina, damaging her uterus, her intestines, and other internal organs. They then dumped her naked on the road and sped off!"

Khadijah dropped her paan and held her chest with a look of horror on her face. The wife of Jaffar who was cleaning the vegetables stared at Selma in shock. Maria, who was reading a Jeffrey Archer book, asked casually, "Will she live?"

"Don't know. The paper just mentions all the celebrities who have voiced their opinion against this cruel and inhumane act," said Selma scanning the paper. "There was a morcha by the Delhi students who demanded justice for Nirbhaya and for other rape victims in India, whose numbers are growing exponentially."

"Is she critical?" asked Maria, placing a bookmark in her book.

"Yes, she seems to be, but she wants to live."

"That's a good sign," Maria said, and Khadijah stared at Maria in disbelief.

"What do you mean by 'that's good'? Are you two elder ones out of your minds?" Khadijah bellowed, hitting Maria on the head. "It's over for that girl. Her izzat is gone. No boy in his right senses will marry her. She will be branded a loose woman for the rest of her life. She will have to live with this shame for the rest of her life. I pray to Khuda that he takes her away and spares her mother and father the dishonor."

Selma glared at her grandmother. "You are definitely insane, Grandmother."

"Hold your tongue!" exclaimed Khadijah.

"No, I will not!" replied Selma, folding the newspaper and placing it in her bag. "Why should Nirbhaya not want or deserve to live? She is not the criminal—she is a victim. She has every right to live with her head held up high with dignity and self-respect. Our society is so hypocritical. The abused gets the punishment, and the abuser is not tarnished. If you want to know my opinion, males are given too much leverage in our society. In this case, they should be dishonored, not Nirbhaya."

"I second the motion," exclaimed Maria, resuming her reading. Khadijah grabbed the book from Maria's hand and tore it. Maria wept ... and Amina wept, remembering her older sister's tears.

The feel of the flute in her hands brought Amina back to reality. Time had passed very quickly. Nirbhaya wanted to live, but she died. There was a candlelight procession, newspaper articles denounced the rapists, there was much talk—but in the end, life continued, and Nirbhaya was forgotten ... Selma was forgotten... Maria was forgotten, but Amina remembered them, and so she wept at last, tears of silent oblation.

However, she wept for another reason as well. Amina wept for Noor, just a few years younger than she was. Noor, who once confided in Amina and told her she wanted to become a photographer. Amina wept for Noor.

For half an hour ago, the quack, Iqbal, Munni, and Natasha had entered the soundproof bedroom and had locked the door. There was an iron rod in the quack's hand.

*

Noor was taken away on a stretcher in the dead of night. Munni and the quack saw to all arrangements. The other occupants of Suliman Manzil did not have a clue about what was going on. Even if they did, they could not question... Bhendi Bazaar was the den of thieves and cut-throats.

Still dressed skimpily in a black brassiere and shorts, Natasha washed the blood off the bedsheets, the sight of her titillating Iqbal.

Amina sat on the floor, watching her so-called husband leer at Natasha. Over the course of time, Amina realized the power Natasha had over Iqbal. If Natasha was not getting her way, all she had to do was to strip for Iqbal, and he would be on her like a wild animal filled with passion and lust.

Once, Amina was washing the dishes in the kitchen when she heard a moaning sound. Thinking it to be a stray cat, she left the dishes and entered the hall to have a look. There she saw Natasha nude humping Iqbal who was kissing her breasts and licking her hard nipples. It was he who was moaning like an animal. Munni was sitting on the sofa right in front of them, smoking a bidi without the least trace of irritation.

It was then Amina realized that she could use the power that Natasha had over Iqbal to her advantage.

After Noor left, Munni tried to coax Iqbal to get Amina to be a sex slave again, but he flatly refused and got himself married to another girl called Bismillah from Malad. She was only fifteen years old.

As Amina played her Casio to the tune of "Jai Kali," a Bollywood song, she made up her mind that she would get out of Iqbal and Munni's clutches once and for all before they thought of using her as a slave again.

Jai Maa Kali, Jai Maa Kali
Jaan Chahe Lenee Pade
Jaan Chahe Denee Pade
Balee ham chadhayenge

All she had to do was to wait for the opportune moment. Natasha, the sex-crazed fool, would aid her indirectly in her escape.

*

While Amina was facing her own troubles at Bhendi Bazaar, the Bandra Reclamation Slum was having a problem of its own. The new state government had come to power after the elections. The leaders of the victorious political parties knew for a fact that the slum dwellers had not voted for them, and therefore they wished to torment them as much as possible where it hurt the most.

The headman, Khan Abdul Mullah, received many letters from the government and municipal corporation, stating that huts and shanties built further into the main road would soon be demolished. Every slum dweller thought nothing of it since they had received similar letters before and nothing ever happened. So, Khan Abdul Mullah decided to ignore the letters as well.

"We have been living here since we left our homes in Bangladesh," shouted the headman at a meeting on the grass fields where the sheep and goats grazed and where the women in burkas drew water from the wells. "We are registered Indians; our homes will not be destroyed. Besides," he continued, gesturing with his hands, "our holy masjid, too, lies near the main road. The government would not dare destroy it, hurting Muslim sentiments that in the bargain may cause a riot. Brothers and Sisters, you all need not fear; our Allah is with us, along with the blessings of his prophet Muhammad. Nothing will happen to our homes."

"Hmm," huffed Khadijah to herself, as she sat on a broken stool in the back row. "Why do I feel that Selma, Allah rest her soul, would think differently at such a moment?"

Tarabai, who was sitting next to her, was smiling, but that smile faded away the very next month, on the seventeenth of January, just two days before the birthday of her first son, Mohan.

On that day, in the early hours of the morning, Tarabai, who was washing some copper utensils outside her hut, heard the sound of tractors, bulldozers, and the screams of someone on the loudspeaker declaring, "Most of these huts have been built too much into the main road. You all were advised to vacate, but you didn't. Therefore, here we are to demolish your illegal huts and shanties."

"We've been living like this for decades!" screamed Khan Abdul Mullah, running towards the bulldozers with shaving cream on his face. He had no time to wipe it off when he heard the sound of the bulldozers. "Get out of here, or we will cause a riot. GET OUT!"

"No chance of that, you old man," the announcer said, smirking into the mike. On that note, the bulldozers started to demolish the huts and shanties that were supposedly obstructing traffic.

Pandemonium broke loose. Tarabai shrieked along with other women, men, and children. One by one clay and brick huts were destroyed, shanties pulled down, and their occupants were running helter-skelter.

"Please, somebody stop them!"

"They are ruining us. Help! Somebody, help!"

"Police! Where are the police? Cease! Stop it! Stop it! Stop it!"

"This is injustice. Political revenge. It is our right to vote for whomever we want."

"Stop! Our homes, where will we go?"

"Why attack the poor? Why don't you attack the rich?"

"Cowards! Help, someone, help!"

"YA ALLAH! OUR MASJID! DON'T YOU DARE!"

However much the residents of the Bandra Reclamation Slum screamed, their houses were destroyed. They crumbled like a pack of cards on a tea table, all in a mess ... one by one. Women in burkas ran with babes in arms; men wailed as their homes were pulled down. Jaffar, half-clad in his lungi, carried Khadijah out of their shanty just before a bulldozer broke it down.

Jaffar looked on, horrified, as he saw the memories of a lifetime in those tin walls crushed under the wheels of the merciless bulldozer. The place where he spent his childhood. The place where his daughters had lived and died... Rahat. Rahat!

"Over my dead body. OVER MY DEAD BODY!"

Jaffar scanned the area to see who was screaming. It was the caretaker, the maulvi, lying on his back in front of the giant wheels of the bulldozer. He was protecting the masjid.

"Tum kya sochate ho? You will destroy our masjid and our community will keep quiet? You will roll your bulldozer over my body, destroy my shrine, and my religious community will remain silent? MERI CHITA KE SAATH SARA MUMBAI JALEGI (along with my dead body, the whole of Mumbai will burn). WHY HAVE YOU STOPPED?" bawled the maulvi, beating his chest as he lay there on the ground. "Start your machine. Kill me along with our Masjid!"

The workers operating the bulldozers looked at one another in fear at last. They did not wish for religious riots to take place. They left the Masjid and the area with their tails between their legs.

The sound of weeping, wailing and crying continued. Tarabai's poorly constructed mud-and-clay hut was now nothing but dust. She beat her breasts and broke her green glass bangles, which pricked her arms causing blood to flow. Khadijah was in a state of shock as she observed her shanty which was nothing more than piles upon piles of broken tin and steel sheets. She did not cry. She did not weep like the other women. She simply stared into space with her head resting on her hand.

The slum became a pile of debris and broken dreams. The passersby in their taxies, buses, swanky cars, rickshaws, and trucks could only stare in disbelief. It looked as if a hurricane blew through the place. No one came to the aid of the slum dwellers. No one wanted to get into trouble with the autocratic government.

Somehow the slum dwellers would have to pick up the pieces left over from the disaster and continue to live, all on their own.

It was not Jaffar who telephoned Amina, but Shantaram, whose shanty had also been crushed to a pulp. He called Suliman Manzil from a P.C.O., as his mobile had been damaged during the demolishing. It was he who informed Amina of her family's loss.

After she handed Iqbal's cell phone back to him at Bhendi Bazaar, she cried silent tears for her father and grandmother. It broke Iqbal's heart to see his so-called wife eschew her musical instruments the whole day and instead weep, covering her face with the palms of her hands. He tried to hold her in his arms, the first act of intimacy he'd offered in over two-and-a-half years, but Amina pushed him away. He did not press himself upon her.

Although Amina wept that whole week, by the end of the night of the seventh day, she knew that if she fled from Suliman Manzil, then she would not be able to return to the Bandra Reclamation Slum as she did not want to be a burden. No! She could not possibly go there, but where else could she go?

It was then that a flicker of memory long wrapped in the folds of her mind unfurled, revealing to her the place she needed to go to—and fast—or worse days endure.

*

After cleaning the soundproof bedroom and cleansing the tied-up Bismillah's private parts, Amina closed the door behind herself and saw Munni's bunch of keys on the hall table. But where was Munni?

As Amina scanned the room, Munni emerged from the kitchen, her bony hands pressed against her flat wrinkly stomach, and she retched on the floor of the hall. The blood she threw up was dark red.

Amina figured that Munni's smoking had at last damaged her lungs and now she was vomiting blood because of it. If she were not taken to a hospital soon enough, she would surely die. Munni must have placed the bunch of keys on the table when she became ill.

Munni again retched, and this time she slipped on her blood and fell face down into the mess. "Amina ladki," she whimpered. "Help, help me."

Amina was in no mood to help. She grabbed hold of the keys swiftly, without Munni realizing it, then found the key to open the main door and threw the bunch of keys back on the table. She clasped the key into her hand. Munni vomited more blood onto the floor and upon herself. She looked as if she were swimming in blood.

Amina wondered where Iqbal was. He had not left the house at all today, and she certainly did not want to confront him on the stairs. She, therefore, walked on the tips of her toes towards the kitchen and peeked in.

There she saw Iqbal naked pressing the completely nude Natasha to the kitchen wall, penetrating her with force, which made the girl moan in ecstasy. They kissed passionately, ignoring Munni's whimpering in the hall.

Natasha licked Iqbal's lips feverishly. "Do it again, baby. Show me you are an animal!" Natasha said with a groan. Iqbal rubbed her breasts and her buttocks and began to hump her with ferocity.

With a smile on her face, Amina ran to the main door. This was the day she would escape this terrible house. She only gathered her tin box of musical instruments, her only true friends. She inserted the key into the lock, opening the wooden door without a creak so that Iqbal wouldn't hear her escape.

"What—what are you doing!" blubbered Munni as she attempted to drag herself out of the vomit without much success. Amina was about to run down the stairs when she heard Natasha moaning loudly from the kitchen.

"Show me you are a lion again, honey. Rub my breasts. They are all yours, darling."

Amina stopped in her tracks, thought for two seconds, and dashed inside the soundproof bedroom. She untied the knots that held Bismillah.

"Where—where you're taking me?" asked the surprised girl. Amina quickly slipped a black nightgown upon Bismillah and taking her hand ran out of the soundproof room, out of the ancient sinful three-roomed house, down the stairs, and into the market.

CHAPTER THREE

It was midnight when the young man living on Mohammad Ali Road called for his tea. One of the servants brought it in just the way his young master wanted it, with no sugar and very little milk.

The young man was sitting in the old study, going through some projects that the students doing their first-year in their Masters in Classic Indian Music had submitted. He was going through a certain girl's project about the development of the dance style called "Kathak over the years up to 2015."

As he read through the neatly handwritten project, he heard someone banging on his front door several times.

The young man put down his fountain pen and removed his golden-rimmed glasses.

At this late hour, who could it be? He thought. He bookmarked the project he was going through with a peacock feather.

"Mausi—mausi, please tell your husband to open the door and see who it is. If it is a beggar, please do drive him away with a stick. I've got a lot of work to do."

"Ji chota sahib," said mausi, her voice echoing throughout the old house. The young man sipped his tea gingerly; it was very hot. The pattering of his aunt's feet heading towards the front door sounded. The door creaked open and the young man heard mausi and her husband, the faithful manservant Abe, talking to whomever was there. He sipped his tea again. It burned his tongue. The young man placed it on the study table next to his ink bottle. The voices echoed throughout the house. The young man massaged his aching forehead with his long, slender fingers.

He had been correcting projects since 5:00 p.m. after he had returned home from the Mumbai University. He had taught the first-year music students what composition of Carnatic music contains, after which he lectured the same class on the various instruments that can be used to play Carnatic music, like the Veena, the Chitravina, the Tanpura, the Clarinet, and the Harmonium. Following this, he gave a lecture in the main lecture hall titled "The Ragas Trail: A note on the evolution of the raga." Finally, at long last, he left the university and returned home by train to Mohammad Ali Road with his students' projects and began at once to correct them without even pausing to have dinner.

The young man was still massaging his head when mausi knocked on the study door.

"Come in, mausi," said the young man. The old woman opened the door hastily, worry written all over her face.

"Whatever is the matter, mausi, you look like you've seen a ghost!"

"Sahib," whispered mausi, pointing towards the front door, "Chota Sahib, there are two young girls outside at the threshold, one in a nightgown reeking of urine and the other holding her up wearing a black salwar kameez and carrying a tin box under her arm. They, they say, well, the one with the box says she knew your father, bada sahib. Chota sahib, they have been walking all over this filthy area searching for this house. ... They... they wish to stay with your permission at least for the night if it pleases your worship. ... And another thing, the girl with the tin box said she was Jaffar's third girl, Amina."

"Amina!" exclaimed the young man, after which he dug into his memories for a while. Jaffar ... tea, biscuits and cookies ... father in study ... a chocolate cookie for ... appropriate name ... Amina Ali Sheikh ... third girl... Amina....

"Let them in, mausi," said the young man, rising to his feet to switch on the two tube lights in his study and to switch off his study lamp. "And bring them some tea, biscuits, and cookies to eat."

"Yes, chota sahib. Oye Abe!" she turned on her heels out of the study, screaming to her husband, who was still at the door. "Call them inside into the study. Chota sahib knows them."

The young man was tall, tanned, and slim. He wore a sherwani with pockets and a wheat-colored khadi jacket along with a pair of light brown village-made sandals which he had purchased from the Gandhi handloom shop near Fort area.

He folded his hands and at that very moment, Abe in his white dhoti and coarse kurta with a huge orange tikka on his forehead brought two pale-looking girls into the study. Abe closed the door behind him, and the young man stared at the girls. He did not recognize either of them but realized that the younger one was panting from exhaustion and on the verge of fainting. He motioned the two girls to sit on a sofa near the study's entrance, which they did gladly.

In a stern voice, he said, "Which one of you knew my father and is the third daughter of Jaffarbhai?"

Amina raised her hand awkwardly, and the young man stared at her contemplatively. He then crooked his head sideways when Amina remained silent for a long time.

"Well, then, prove it to me. Prove that you knew my father well."

Amina frowned at the young man while the eager Bismillah raised her hand, looking coaxingly at Amina and sang out from her torn mouth four lines of poetry.

I have lost my voice it has fallen asleep,
When did I rise from my sleep and when
did I awake?
But I will die if I am separated from your holy arms,
I have lost my voice it resides in the
realm of the dead.

The young man stood in place as if he had been stung. The passage that the younger girl had sung was one of Dr. Rahim Muhammad Sheikh's lullabies, his adopted father's lullabies, which he used to sing to him to put him to sleep. It had been taken from his great-great-grandmother's book of poems titled *The Fallen Couplet...* Her name was Amina Ali Sheikh ... Amina ... Amina!

The younger girl, though battered and abused physically, as the young man could see, had a smile on her face as she finished singing and pointed towards Amina.

"She—she used to sing it to—to me," she stammered. "She said her mother, Rahat, taught her these verses when she was just a child staying at the Bandra Reclamation Slum. She, I mean, Amina's mother, Rahat, used to visit your father in this house very often until she died during those bomb blasts eleven years ago."

The young man nodded in recognition at last. So this young girl in a black salwar kameez was Amina, the third daughter of Jaffar, whom he had named in honor of his great-great-grandmother, but why was she so silent? And why was the younger girl so battered up?

"What brings you both here?" asked the young man.

"Er... may I know your name, sir?" stammered the younger girl.

"Dr. Jumman Rahim Sheikh, doctor of music at the Mumbai University."

It was then that Bismillah, the younger girl, narrated to Jumman the tragedy of their lives at Suliman Manzil—the prostitution racket, the abuse, the rapes, the inhuman way in which they were treated by Iqbal and Munni, the human trafficking business, and their escape.

Jumman listened to everything in rapt attention, horrified. He then paced about the study deep in thought. Mausi by then had already brought in a silver tray containing two cups of hot tea, chocolate cookies, and Marie biscuits. She stood outside the study to see if the young Jumman was safe with these strange women.

Bismillah went on to describe how Amina was spared further sexual abuse because she could play her flute, mouth organ, and pipe like a musical genius. That caught Jumman's attention, and he turned his gaze towards the silent Amina.

"So you play some musical instruments very well, eh?"

Amina nodded slowly, a faraway look in her eyes. Jumman pointed towards the box on Amina's lap.

"What's inside there?"

"Her musical instruments," replied Bismillah hastily. She then nudged Amina who very mechanically opened the box, revealing to Jumman her only material treasures.

Jumman lifted the pipe from the tin box and examined it.

At this time, Bismillah told Jumman that neither of them wished to return to their mother's homes. Instead, they wished to stay in a hostel for girls where Bismillah would be able to find work and study further, while Amina wished to join a musical academy. They did not want to report anything of their sexual abuse to the police.

The doctor of music raised his eyes from the pipe in his hands after Bismillah concluded her rapid monologue. He believed them, but he wanted to be sure. He placed the pipe back in the tin box, went to his study chair, and lowered himself upon his seat.

He cleared his throat before he addressed them. "The tea will get cold and the biscuits soft. Please do nourish yourselves, for we have a lot to discuss concerning this very serious matter."

Like savages, both girls gobbled down whatever lay on the silver tray. They licked their fingers after they finished. Jumman then ordered mausi to bring the girls some bread, butter, and jam along with some milk, which she did in a jiffy. The malnourished girls ate up all that too, again unceremoniously licking their fingers.

Bismillah, while she ate, spoke a lot to Jumman, cursing her family for letting her get married to an unknown stranger right after her tenth-grade exams when she wanted to continue her education, go to college, and get a job in a regular office. The doctor nodded at her every statement, but his mind was focused on Amina, the silent one.

Mausi came back to take the tray away. As she pattered her way to the upstairs kitchen, Jumman pointed towards Amina's bandaged earlobe.

"What's that, now?"

Bismillah answered him yet again, "A disgusting taxi driver chewed the flesh of her earlobe while he was ... was ... was with her, and they wouldn't send her to a regular doctor because of the possible repercussions, so, you know, they asked a quack to bandage it up." She cracked her fingers, looking towards Amina, coaxing her to say something, but Amina clung to the tin box in her lap in silence.

The young doctor raised an eyebrow for a while and then lowered it.

With the kindest tone he could muster, he addressed Amina: "I can understand, Amina, what you have gone through, but being quiet and not speaking at all will cause further damage to your precious self. Come on, Amina, say something!"

Amina remained silent but her eyes began to well up with tears, which rolled down her fair pink cheeks.

Jumman adjusted himself on his seat and addressed her again. "Please say something. Do you want to press charges against Iqbal and Munni?"

Amina shook her head very slowly with a blurred look in her eyes.

"Do you want me to call your father to talk to you?" he asked.

Again, she shook her head. And Jumman leaned back in his chair, thinking to himself, *Why doesn't she talk?*

Bismillah shook Amina's shoulder. "Amina didi, please talk to Jumman, sir, er ... I mean Dr. Jumman," she corrected herself. "Say something, Amina. SAY SOMETHING—ANYTHING!"

Amina remained as silent as the grave.

Bismillah began to weep. The doctor thought for a moment and came up with an idea.

"Okay, okay, listen," said Jumman, lifting up the palms of his hands. "You don't want to talk, and that's fine with me, but Bismillah says you want to join a musical academy, right? Well, then you've got three instruments with you in your tin box," and as he said it, he leaned back comfortably in his chair, his fingers interlocked with one another. "Pick anyone you wish, and play a tune that fully describes what you are feeling right now." He smiled kindly. "Go ahead, prove to me that you are a musician."

Amina stared at Jumman for a moment. She then stared into her tin box, deliberated for a moment and picked up her favorite instrument ... her flute.

Bismillah beamed with torn lips. Dr. Jumman Rahim Sheikh raised both his eyebrows.

With her eyes open, Amina put the flute to her mouth, shocking Jumman when she started to play a rather complicated raga.

The doctor of music stared in wonder as Amina's fingers moved along the flute like a professional player. The mood of the raga was one of pain, the kind of pain that heals outwardly but leaves the insides scarred; the kind of pain that only the bearer or victim knows and yet is silent about it; the kind of pain a mother feels when she gives birth to her baby and then dies due to exhaustion.

Bismillah cried as the raga continued while Jumman's eyes lit on fire. *A prodigy,* he thought to himself *a musical prodigy.* ... He had never heard such music in his life ... the raga ... such a novel raga of pain.

Amina's woeful raga lasted fifteen minutes, precisely how ancient Carnatic Ragas ended, and then she began on the same note to play a song.

Jumman found the song to be familiar, but he couldn't place it in his mind, because Amina was playing it so beautifully.

Seeing Jumman's bafflement, Bismillah, who like Amina had been educated in a Catholic Convent School, began to sing to the tune of the Christian hymn that Amina was playing.

Were you there when they crucified my Lord
Were you there?
Were you there when they crucified my Lord
Were you there?
Oh – oh - oh
Sometimes, it causes me to tremble – tremble –
tremble
Were you there when they crucified my Lord
Were you there?

When Jumman recognized the song, his chin quivered on the verge of breaking down in sobs, but he controlled himself. Hearing the enchanting music, mausi and her husband, Abe, and the other three manservants stood at the threshold of the study, listening in amazement.

Were you there when they nailed him to a tree
Were you there?
Were you there when they nailed him to a tree
Were you there?
Oh – oh – oh
Sometimes, it causes me to tremble – tremble –

tremble
Were you there when they nailed him to a tree
Were you there?

The servants lowered their heads and mausi began to weep. The doctor of music, being what he was, checked every note, every single musical note. They were all perfect and accurate, and this nineteen-year-old girl had learned all this by ear. *What would happen when she goes to music school?* Jumman thought, clenching his teeth so that he would not cry in front of his servants. This... this was the girl that had been used by men? This ... this was the girl that had not been allowed to develop her talent? This ... this was Amina? Rahat's third girl child! Bismillah with both her hands caught hold of her vagina, remembering her months of torture and humiliation, while her mouth continued to sing.

Were you there when they laid him in the tomb
Were you there?
Were you there when they laid him in the tomb
Were you there?
Oh – Oh – Oh
Sometimes, it causes me to tremble – tremble – tremble
Were you there when they laid him in the tomb
Were you there?

Amina ended the hymn with an extended note and then like Bismillah, she caught hold of her vagina, placed the flute hastily into the tin box, rolled off the sofa onto the floor, and began to wail in pain.

*

As she stood backstage, Amina remembered her mother's words.

"Dekhna, Selma. One day my Amina will perform at a concert. Dr. Rahim Muhammad Sheikh Sahib has promised me so!"

"Whatever you say, ammi!" Selma would say while she fried the chapattis for dinner. "Ek baat bolu, ammi? Why is your tape record stuck only on that one topic, 'My Amina will perform at a concert'?"

"Yeah, ammi!" added Maria who was cradling Afsheen in her arms. "Why do you give so much leverage to Amina? She is a girl, too, just like all of us."

"Rubbish!" Rahat, the wife of Jaffar, would say. "Have you heard her playing her flute? Ya Allah, her music sounds like the soothing sound of a cooing baby."

"Yeah!" grumbled Selma, "Except Afsheen and Feroza have never *cooed* in their lives, and neither did Maria when she was a baby—one and all, always bawling!"

"Ammi, dekh phir se mujhe chidah rahi hai," screamed Maria in imitation, which woke up the toddler Feroza who was sleeping on the lap of her mother, and she began to cry. Rahat tried to put Feroza back to sleep with no effect.

"You see," said Selma triumphantly, "this is a family problem, I tell you, tears, tears, tears; women in India only shed tears!"

Immediately hearing her sister cry, Afsheen would also begin to bawl in Maria's arms.

"Stop crying, you idiot," Maria would scold Afsheen, but she wouldn't stop crying. Selma would wink at her sister Amina, who would be clearing her pipe with a hand-kerchief, sitting next to her grandmother Khadijah.

"Ya Khuda! Give the children to me!" Khadijah yelled, extending her hands. "I'll shut both of them up."

When Feroza and Afsheen reached Khadijah's lap, she slapped them several times on their smooth cheeks, and they shut up immediately.

"Look now," teased Selma, putting some ghee on the frying pan. "That's how girls are treated all the time. When they are crying, hit them. When they are growing up, hit them. When they want to study, hit them. When they want to ..."

"Shut up!" Khadijah growled. "You talk too much for your age. Hold your tongue. Remember, you're in the midst of elders."

Selma had let the chapatti burn purposely that day so that it could be reserved for Khadijah. As usual, Amina and Jaffar got the best ghee-laden chapattis.

Amina remembered all this, her sisters Selma, Maria, Feroza, and Afsheen, and her mother, Rahat, with fondness. Oh, how different life would have been if they were all alive. Still, she knew in her heart that wherever they were, they were praying for her well-being constantly.

Amina clutched her flute, this time it was a silver aluminum flute, rich and expensive, as she stood backstage where the grand Carnatic Musical was going on. Ten years had passed since her gallant escape from Iqbal's chawl.

"Nervous?" asked Dr. Jumman Rahim Sheikh, standing beside her. Amina shook her head in reply. Where music was concerned, Amina had never been nervous. When it came to music, she felt that she was born to be one with it.

"That's good," whispered Jumman. "After ten years of training, this is your big day, Amina. Make the most of it."

Amina looked towards Jumman with a smile that seemed to say thank you, and yes, I am going to make the most of it, and yes, this is my big day, all at the same time. *I wish ammijaan were here to see me on stage*, she thought.

Amina's heart was racing. She was so excited to play at last to an audience who would appreciate her and her music, and her soul.

Bismillah stood next to Jumman. She stayed by Amina's side always as a token of her gratitude. For if it were not for Amina, Bismillah would still be in the sex trade and may have been killed the way Noor had been. But no! Amina, the silent one, had saved her.

As all three of them peeked through the drawn curtains to the main stage, they saw the maestros of Carnatic music: Pandit Shivaji Raj Patel on the sitar, Pandit Mudra Singh Kang on the sarangi, and Ustad Jeevan Lal on the tabla, the three of them performing the medieval Carnatic player Muthuswami Dikshitar's *Navagraha* to an enthralled audience consisting of musicians, music lovers, patrons of music, film stars, theater celebrities, personalities, politicians, historians, and families of the musicians playing on the stage.

In the audience, somewhere in the third row, sat Jaffar and his now deaf-and-blind mother, Khadijah. She couldn't hear the beautiful music clearly, but she wanted to be there for the event. She could not see except for a bit of light and shadows, but she came. ... She came for her Amina, the third daughter of Jaffar, whom she had unknowingly sent into the den of the devil. Yes, she came seeking forgiveness. Next to Jaffar, Shantaram sat teary-eyed.

"Our Amina bacchi will be better and bigger than any Bollywood actor today," he said, sniffling into Jaffar's ears. "I'll never forgive myself for sending her off with that, that *monster,* Iqbal..."

"Let the past be buried," Jaffar said, his eyes glued to the stage. "She will be appearing on the stage now at any moment."

Shantaram blew his nose into his handkerchief and wiped his tears of remorse with his fingers. As he placed his kerchief on his thigh, he became nostalgic remembering the eight-year-old Amina at the Bandra Reclamation Slum sitting upon a heap of wet garbage and in her white school uniform and tight white hijab, playing Bollywood songs on her wooden flute while the street urchins played and danced all around her as if she were a pied piper or Lord Krishna with his gopis.

The old electrician and matchmaker also remembered the time when Amina, the little Amina, used to play with her best friend, Nirmala, the unwanted daughter of Tarabai. They would slip over grease and sewage, hide in filthy dustbins, and help milk the cows at the cowshed. They would help the owner of the cowshed make cow dung cakes to be used as fuel to light his home at night. They would giggle when one of the other girls would slip and fall on a piece of human excreta, which covered the whole length of the slum. Yes, Shantaram remembered them fondly, the two inseparable best friends of old: Amina, a Muslim, and Nirmala, a Hindu.

"Look, look, Shantaramji!" exclaimed Jaffar, pointing towards the stage. "They are finishing. It will be Amina's turn next."

Jaffar then shook his mother gently and said in a loud voice that angered some members of the audience, "Sunte ho, ammi? Our Amina is playing her solo next!"

"Kya, kya, kya?" Khadijah replied so loudly that the Bollywood actor Rishi Kapoor, sitting in front of them, turned his head towards them in irritation.

"Will you two please keep quiet?" the veteran actor commanded. "We have come to hear some decent music, not your screaming."

In answer, Shantaram pointed towards the stage saying, "Sir, you do not know that all these fellows on stage who are playing their fiddles are nothing compared to our Amina, who is coming up next. I tell you, sir, she plays the flute like Lord Krishna himself!"

"Hmmm," murmured the actor. "We'll see about that, but silence now."

"Yes, yes sir," stuttered Jaffar, shushing Shantaram harshly with his gaze.

The *Navagraha* ended. The experienced and well-known musicians were given a hearty round of applause to which they all bowed low and kissed their instruments jointly, taking the name of the Hindu goddess Saraswati, the goddess of music.

Shabana Azmi, another well-known Bollywood actress, came to the podium, adjusted the mike, and said, "That was a mesmerizing piece from the masters of Carnatic Music themselves. It is always a joy to hear them play. These musicians have surpassed our expectations yet again by performing the *Navagraha* of his reverence Muthuswami Dikshitar who was born in 1776 and was one of the most respected musicians of his time. His works are a blend, as you all well know, of organized lyrics, majestic melody, and grand themes.

"His astonishing intelligence and scholarship are revealed in all his works. His creations reveal the impact of Hindustani and Western music on..."

Shantaram grumbled as his heartbeat began to throb in his throat. "Jaldi karo! Enough of the musician's biography. We want to see and hear our Amina, our silent one!"

Jaffar smiled weakly as Rishi Kapoor again turned and glared at all three of them before turning back to listen to Shabana Azmi.

Khadijah could barely hear a word the actress of yesteryear was saying. She pulled out some paan leaves from her old purse and stuffed them into her mouth, chewing the betel leaves with relish.

"What is this, ammi?" admonished Jaffar, as the stench of the betel leaves diffused through the air-conditioned hall. "Why did you have to chew your paan now?"

"Kya, kya, kya?"

"Your paan —"

"Hai kya yeh daam?"

"Not 'daam,' ammi, 'paan' – **PAAN**!"

"Khan?" replied a confused Khadijah, looking around her, quite perplexed. "But Aamir Khan is not sitting here, beta; he is sitting near the stage in front ... I think.... It could be Shahrukh Khan also, though ... can't make out a thing with these eyes of mine."

"Not 'Khan,' ammi, your paan, *paan*!"

"Kya, kya, kya?"

Jaffar hit his forehead with his left palm while Rishi Kapoor counted from one to twenty to calm himself.

It was after a full fifteen minutes that the biography of Muthuswami Dikshitar was finished and then Shabana Azmi declared, "And now, ladies and gentlemen, presenting to you the new generation of Carnatic music players. A twenty-nine-year-old woman and protégé of Dr. Jumman Rahim Sheikh will be playing for us right now on the flute. She has selected Oothukkadu Venkata Kavi's piece called *Vande Valmiki Kokilam*, which is a treatise on the writer of the Ramayana, the revered Saint Valmiki. Please put your hands together for Miss Amina Patel. I repeat, Miss Amina!"

Bismillah and Jumman clapped together along with the audience.

"Go for it, Amina!" said Jumman, as Amina drew open the velvet purple curtains and strode to the center of the stage with confidence. Jaffar could not control his tears as he observed Amina. She was wearing a dark green nylon hijab that exposed her beautiful face, a long black coat, green socks and black sandals. Her hands were only exposed from her wrist. Amina bowed to the audience and held the flute to her mouth, ready to play.

"This is it," whispered Jumman to Bismillah excitedly.

"Well, this is it!" whispered Shantaram, adjusting his glasses on the bridge of his nose as he sat in the audience.

"Kya, kya, kya?"

"This better be good," groaned Rishi Kapoor massaging his head.

Amina looked towards Pandit Shivaji Raj Patel on the sitar to give her the starting note. With a gentle smile, the master strummed Kakali Nishadam – N_3 Carnatic chord, which in Western music meant the B^6 chord (flat). Amina was about to play the first note when suddenly she looked at the audience and grew pale.

"What happened?" asked Jumman backstage, looking to see why Amina had stopped.

"Now what's up?" grumbled Rishi Kapoor, pointing towards the stage. "Why has she frozen in place?"

Indeed, Amina had frozen in place—not because she had forgotten her notes, but because several police officers had entered the auditorium. The audience and the musicians onstage stared at them.

"What's going on out there?" shouted Jumman, drawing the curtains apart and striding towards the center of the stage. "Why are you policemen here?" he asked aloud, while the musicians onstage began to stare at one another in mute incomprehension.

"Kya, kya, kya?" questioned the confused Khadijah, shaking Jaffar's shoulder. "Why is my Rahat's third daughter not playing her blasted flute?"

Jaffar and Shantaram's faces twisted in rage as two constables escorted Iqbal in filthy prison clothes into the auditorium.

"How dare you bring that beast in here!" shrieked Jumman, clutching hold of Amina, who shivered, hiding her pale face in Jumman's chest. "Get him out of her."

"Excuse me, doctor sahib," said an inspector in a polite but commanding tone of voice. "We have not come here to disrupt your peaceful gathering, but we are bound by an oath."

"What bloody oath?" snarled Jumman.

"The last wish of a prisoner who is to be hanged to death for murder," declared the inspector loudly for the whole audience to hear. "We policeman of Mumbai and India before hanging a person condemned to death must fulfill, if possible, his or her last request."

He then pointed to Iqbal whose head was bowed low. "This man Iqbal Muhammad Merchant will be hanged to-night at the gallows. His last request was that—"

"That what, for heaven's sake?" screamed Rishi Kapoor from the audience. "This whole show has become like a soap opera that my wife watches at home."

The inspector cleared his throat before he spoke again in an authoritative voice.

"The last wish of prisoner number 370, who is Iqbal Muhammad Merchant, is to hear one last time his ... er, ex-wife, Amina, play the flute for him, after which he shall give up his life."

A hush fell over the audience. Amina raised her eyes and looked towards the entrance of the stage. There, in black-and-white stripes, with a long beard and a wrinkled face, stood Iqbal with tears in his eyes. Jumman let go of Amina but stood behind her.

Iqbal put his palms together and said, "Please, Amina, one last time before they kill me. One ... last ... song ..."

Amina wiped her tears and swallowed the mucous that was forming in her throat. She motioned Pandit Shivaji Patel to play the chord B^6 (flat) again. He did so. With her eyes fixed on Iqbal, Amina began to play *Vande Valmiki Kokilam.*

The music was heavenly, and Rishi Kapoor's jaw dropped in shock just the way Iqbal's jaw had dropped eleven years ago.

To the veteran actor, the music sounded like all the angels of heaven were playing their flutes to soothe the soul of the dying criminal. At once, Rishi Kapoor felt that Lord Rama was dancing with his beautiful wife, Sita, in a palace of gold, and in another moment, he felt that his soul was transported to the realm of the sage Valmiki when he, by the side of a babbling brook, inked on banana leaves the story of Lord Rama. What music ... what heavenly music!

Jumman bowed his head low as Amina played with her heart and her soul. She played as she had never played before.

As she played, the sarangi pandit, the sitar pandit and the tabla ustad accompanied her with tears in their eyes. When the song reached its peak and when Rishi Kapoor felt that the Himalayas were calling out to the snow to bestow on them the gift of rivers so holy, he uttered these words:

My lover has come to bid me farewell,
To Lord Yama now will my everlasting dwell.
I am a moth singed by the flame of desire,
To you dear one I owe a couplet but oh what music
you make!

Bismillah cried bitterly, while Amina played feverishly, her fingers so delicately singing her tears to the heavens.

When it ended, Amina rushed back into Jumman's arms and wept, while the audience gave her a standing ovation, screaming, "Encore! Encore! Amina, once more, once more!"

Iqbal, whose legs and wrists were chained, bowed low, and then, with the inspector and the other policemen, left the auditorium.

***

ABOUT THE AUTHOR

Fiza Pathan has a bachelor's degree in arts from the University of Mumbai, where she majored in history and sociology with a first class. She also has a bachelor's degree in education, again with a first class, her special subjects being English and history.

Fiza has written eleven award-winning books and a short story, which reflect her interest in furthering the cause of education and in championing social issues. In more than seventy literary competitions, she has placed either as the winner or a finalist, chief among them the Digital Book World 2018 Awards, Killer Nashville 2018 Silver Falchion Award, 2018 Purple Dragonfly Book Awards, Montaigne Medal (2018 Eric Hoffer Book Award), Readers' Favorite Book Awards, Reader Views Literary Awards, Eric Hoffer Book Award, Foreword Reviews Indie Fab Book Awards, Mom's Choice Awards, Literary Classics Book Awards, and Dan Poynter's Global E-book Awards. She lives with her maternal family and writes novels and short stories in most genres.

Twitter handle @FizaPathan

Amazon link:

http://www.amazon.com/Fiza-Pathan/e/B0091BCNTU

Website: https://fizapathanpublishing.ink/

www.ingramcontent.com/pod-product-compliance
Lightning Source LLC
LaVergne TN
LVHW091458170726
843492LV00001B/242